Dear Reader,

You're about to experience a revolution in reading—BookShots.

BookShots are a whole new kind of book—100 percent story-driven, no fluff, always under $5.

I've written or co-written nearly all the BookShots and they're among my best n vels of any length.

At 150 pages or fewer, BookShots can be read in a night, on a commute, or even on your cell phone during breaks at work.

I hope you enjoy *The Exile*.

All my best,

James Patterson

P.S.

For special offers and the full list of BookShots titles, please go to
BookShots.com

BOOK**SHOTS**

- [ ] *The Shut-In* (with Duane Swierczynski)
- [ ] *After the End* (with Brendan DuBois)
- [ ] *Diary of a Succubus* (with Derek Nikitas)
- [ ] *Detective Cross* (by James Patterson)
- [ ] *Private: Gold* (with Jassy Mackenzie)
- [ ] *The Lawyer Lifeguard* (with Doug Allyn)
- [ ] *Stingrays* (with Duane Swierczynski)
- [ ] *Steeplechase* (with Scott Slaven)
- [ ] *Nooners* (with Tim Arnold)
- [ ] *The Medical Examiner* (with Maxine Paetro)
- [ ] *The Dolls* (with Kecia Bal)
- [ ] *Dead Man Running* (with Christopher Farnsworth)
- [ ] *Stealing Gulfstreams* (with Max DiLallo)
- [ ] *You've Been Warned—Again* (with Howard Roughan)
- [ ] *Scott Free* (with Rob Hart)
- [ ] *Manhunt* (with James O. Born)

BOOKSHOTS
Flames

THE EXILE

JAMES PATTERSON
WITH ALISON JOSEPH

BOOK**SHOTS**

Little, Brown and Company

New York Boston London

Copyright © 2017 JBP Business, LLC
Excerpt from *Manhunt* copyright © 2017 JBP Business, LLC

BookShots / Little, Brown and Company
Hachette Book Group
1290 Avenue of the Americas, New York, NY 10104
bookshots.com

First North American Edition: November 2017
Originally published in Great Britain by Random House UK, March 2017

BookShots is an imprint of Little, Brown and Company, a division of Hachette Book Group, Inc. The Little, Brown name and logo are trademarks of Hachette Book Group, Inc. The BookShots name and logo are trademarks of JBP Business, LLC.

The publisher is not responsible for websites (or their content) that are not owned by the publisher.

The Hachette Speakers Bureau provides a wide range of authors for speaking events. To find out more, go to hachettespeakersbureau.com or call (866) 376-6591.

ISBN 978-0-316-41110-3
LCCN 2017945662

10 9 8 7 6 5 4 3 2 1

LSC-C

Printed in the United States of America

THE EXILE

PROLOGUE

IN THE TOWN OF Kilmeaden in Ireland, just west of Galway, on a rainy October night, little Bobby O'Connor was lying fast asleep in his warm bed. His mother, Bridie, went up to check on him. She stood in the doorway, watching his breathing, his peaceful sleep. She reflected on the quiet contentment of her life, just herself and her little boy.

She went back downstairs and picked up her sewing, listening to the rain hammering against the windows.

Then another sound…A cry from upstairs, a thump, and then Bobby's footsteps, fast pad-padding down the stairs. He appeared in the doorway, white as a sheet, terrified.

Bridie sprang to her feet. "What is it?" she asked him, gathering him into her arms. "My boy, whatever is the matter?"

He could hardly speak. Eventually he managed, "He had a green mask. Like leaves. And he was singing. A horrid, horrid song, like a lion growling…"

This hit Bridie like a punch to the guts. "Who?" she asked, but she knew the answer.

"In the window," the little boy said. "I heard the singing. I woke up. And then I saw him through the window. I called for you—the man was laughing. I ran, I ran downstairs...." He burst into tears.

"Hush now, little one," she said, holding him close. "You're safe now. It was a bad dream. Nothing but a dream."

She took him upstairs to her big double bed and lay down next to him. Soon he settled back to sleep.

Bridie lay awake, trembling.

A bad dream, she thought. *If only it was.*

As soon as dawn broke, she picked up her phone and dialed a number.

CHAPTER 1

IN A TALL, SLEEK, glass tower block in the City of London, Finn O'Grady heard his phone ring. The pink of the new day tinted the City landscape, catching the watery flicker of the Thames. O'Grady had been sitting, watching the CCTV screens of the sleeping buildings, waiting for his night shift to end.

He looked at his phone.

Bridie O'Connor.

He almost didn't answer it. But it was six in the morning and she'd been in his thoughts for most of the night. Like every night. Even though he hadn't seen her for three and a half years. Three years, six months. And eight days.

"Hi," he said, his voice neutral.

"Thank God." Her voice was a sigh of relief.

"What is it?"

"It's here," she said. "Oh, Finn, thank God you answered. I didn't know who else to call, who else would understand…."

"What's here?"

"You know what. Bobby saw it in the night, at his window. I told him it was a bad dream. He believed me last night. He won't believe me when it happens again."

O'Grady was silent.

"You've got to come back," she said.

"You know I can't."

"But—the curse. We need you...." Her voice caught in a sob.

"That's an old tale. An old folk story..."

"Finn, please believe me."

"I promised I'd never come back. And I keep my promises."

"What about another promise you made once?"

"I'm an exile, Bridie."

"It's an exile you chose, Finn. And you can choose to end it."

The call clicked off.

Finn O'Grady stared at his phone in the rosy autumnal dawn.

CHAPTER 2

THE SLEEK TOWERS OF the City of London glittered in the first rays of the sun. In front of O'Grady sat a bank of CCTV cameras, flickering grimy images.

This is what I've become, he thought. *I was the top cop in Galway—now I'm watching warehouses storing computer kit. And all because I held out for the truth, for justice.*

"An exile you chose," she'd said.

He got to his feet, paced up and down.

And if I'd chosen otherwise? What would it be like? To have a home, a garden, a potato patch. A wife…

He stopped his pacing. He remembered his mother's words as he played out in the back yard when he was a boy. "I won't be keeping you here, Finn boy," she'd say. "A nomad, that's what you are. A restless spirit. You belong to the whole world, not to me."

A nomad, he thought. *Belonging nowhere.*

O'Grady gazed out of the wide, bright window.

A night watchman, paid to guard the wealth of companies against those who would try to take it.

How far from my mother's dream of warriorhood, of might and right.

And now this…

He stared at his phone.

In his mind, the pleading, desperate voice of Bridie O'Connor.

"It's here," she'd said.

He knew what she meant. The Salter curse, which came through her father's line, before she married into the O'Connors. Bridie's grandfather, James Salter, was English. He was said to have stolen land in Galway that had belonged to an Irish family. At the time the locals had a story of the ancient Green Man. They believed he would protect them from the English incomers. The Green Man was invincible. In the ancient folk song they try to kill him by earth, air, fire and water, but he always rises up again.

James Salter showed no interest in the stories. He expanded the farm, ignored the locals, claimed he didn't give a damn what these inbred savages thought of him.

His only son, Richard—Bridie's father—was different. Richard was a gentle soul, a solitary child who grew up to be an academic—a historian at the university. Much loved locally, he seemed to carry the guilt of the stolen land, the opposite of his bully of a father.

It wasn't surprising that old Salter was unpopular. Nor was it surprising that the locals used these tales to express their sense of injustice.

What was surprising was that decades later, at Bridie's window, her little boy had seen something resembling the Green Man of the stories.

O'Grady was brought back from his thoughts by a crash of doors and a beep of security gates.

"All right?" Mo and Ahmed tumbled through the doors and thumped tubs of hot coffee onto their desks. "Quiet night?"

"Quiet night," O'Grady agreed, handing over a large bunch of keys. Mo was bearded and trim; Ahmed was tall and broad-shouldered, his shirt tight over his muscles. O'Grady sometimes wondered what they made of him, with his ten years on them.

He said his farewells and went down the back stairs into the yard. The huge steel gate slid open to let him out.

His flat was in East London, two dingy rooms on a road which never slept. The dusty windows let in minimal daylight and the warring aromas from the artisanal bakers and the cheap fried chicken shop below.

O'Grady took off his jacket. He pulled a comb through his chestnut-brown hair. A glance in the mirror showed a tall, muscular figure, clean-shaven, blue-eyed.

A cowboy, Bridie had once called him. "You calling me names?" he'd asked. "No," she'd laughed, shaking her head. "From the Westerns, the old films. You look like a man who's got what it takes. That's what I mean."

He looked at the image in front of him. He wondered what Bridie would see now.

He slept fitfully, dreaming of Ireland. Dreaming of Bridie, remembering their happy times before she married Stuart, before little Bobby came along.

At four in the afternoon he woke, got up, boiled the kettle, made tea. He sat at his table, stirring the spoon around in his mug.

Bridie would be wanting an answer. But what could he say to her?

A nomad, my mother would call me, before I knew the meaning of the word. "A warrior," she'd say, watching me playing in the dust. "One of the ancients."

I was her beloved only child. Running round the yard with my wooden sword, slaying dragons. Important work, I thought at the time. The dragons were real enough to me.

And then I grew up, fell in love. But I'd catch Bridie watching me as my mother had, as if she too was thinking that one day she would have to let me go.

And then came the time when she said to me, "I'm a woman who needs to be a mother. I need to find the man who'll give me that."

Soon after, Stuart O'Connor appeared on the scene with his fancy motorbike, a Suzuki Intruder, bought from a dealer in Raheen who turned out to have stolen it. But Bridie was happy enough being whisked along the country lanes.

The last time he'd seen Bridie had been in the yard at Caffrey's stables, a set of reins looped over one arm, little Bobby toddling at her feet, her brother Mikey in the distance shoveling manure.

She'd gone up to him, looked into his eyes, taken hold of his hand. She was about to speak.

Stay. Don't go.

He'd waited for the words.

Instead, she'd shaken her head, squeezed his hand, then turned and walked away.

She didn't look back.

He'd taken the next flight to London.

O'Grady checked his phone, picked up the address of that night's job from his company.

As the sun set across London, he made his way back to the City, back towards the river. He thought about the fields beneath his feet, the medieval markets, the Roman wine cellars and garrison stations. He looked upwards at the brand-new towers of shimmering glass.

By ten o'clock, he was sitting alone on the back stairs of a storage company. He could feel his pistols, Glock 17s, one in each pocket. It was a cool clear night and he sat out of sight, by the metal fencing of the warehouse yard.

The night was quiet. Just the occasional plane, its tiny dotted lights against the sky. He could hear Bridie's voice in his head: "I didn't know who else to call...."

He felt a wave of rage.

Bridie wants me to be what I used to be, the man she could rely on.

The moon had risen, a perfect crescent. He wondered if they could see the same moon in Galway.

CHAPTER 3

MIKEY SALTER STARED UP at the perfect crescent moon as it rose behind Tynan's bar, down the lane from the stable yard where he worked. He walked to his car, steadily enough, he thought, one foot landing safely in front of the other. It's not as if anyone's going to know.

Start the engine, pull out of the pub car park, put on the radio, Bowie, isn't it? "Golden Years..." He found himself singing along as he pushed the car up a gear and sped around the bends in the dark lane.

"Mikey, you've had enough," Griff the landlord had said, two or three pints before. But the old country lane was familiar, and anyway, who else was going to be on it at that time of night?

Something reared up in the darkness, across the road. A block. A tree, he realized, as he jammed on the brakes and felt the tires spin. The car swerved and stopped, inches from collision.

"Now what?" Mikey Salter said, out loud. He got out of his car. A huge tree trunk, right across the road. How the devil had it got there?

It was a still night, with an autumnal chill in the air. The crescent moon was crisp against the dark sky.

Then he heard it. A weird, guttural singing, a deep voice. A song, sounded like Gaelic, he thought, like the old folk songs his dad used to play on those funny old recordings. It seemed familiar, but he couldn't quite put his finger on it.

A step, a crunch of a boot behind him. He turned and faced the barrel of a shotgun, glinting in the moonlight.

Then noise, an explosion of pain, the tearing of bullets, of guts.

The last thing Mikey Salter saw was a mask of green leaves in the ghostly moonlight, a face grinning behind its beard of twigs. The last thing he heard was the humming of the strange song, the low growling notes, as a cloud descended and his breath rattled out of him.

Then, nothing.

CHAPTER 4

FINN O'GRADY SAT IN the shabby office of the storage company. The moon had softened, lowered into clouds, and was now just a patch of grainy light against the City towers.

Suddenly there was a flash of light outside. The security beam had been triggered.

He was quickly on his feet, a hand in each pocket, the steel of the pistols under his fingers.

He could hear the click of the gates.

Silently, he stepped to the wall and stood hidden in the darkness of the office.

Then a noise. A drill, was it? Someone trying to get through the locks.

He scanned the CCTV. Scratchy images panned across shadowy corners, showing nothing at all.

O'Grady slipped out of the office. He stood at the top of the stairs, motionless, invisible.

A wisp of a movement across the yard. Three figures in the darkness, scaling the gates. The searchlights flashed across their hooded faces, but they moved fast, reaching the top and then jumping softly into the yard, bolting towards the storage units.

The beam of light cut across the space around them, but they were hidden now.

O'Grady could hear the clicks of equipment, the hard screech of drills applied to metal crates.

He pulled out his guns—one right, one left—and stepped down the staircase, emerging into the light.

"Stop," he called out. "Stop right there."

Three figures whirled and faced him, three blank hoods, six holes for expressionless eyes.

There was a dead silence. Three male faces stared. Then there was the click of a gun.

O'Grady fired a split second before the lad did. A bullet cracked into the wall above O'Grady's head, but O'Grady's aim was true. The young man dropped to the ground. His Skorpion 9mm slid across the yard, glinting in the security light. Around him was panic, shouting, cursing, running back towards the gates.

O'Grady touched the remote and the delivery gates glided open. Two hooded figures tumbled through it.

They found themselves facing the security doors.

Then O'Grady touched his remote again and the gates slid shut, cutting off their exit.

They began to shout. O'Grady could hear their cursing, their cries, the rattle of steel as they kicked the doors. He smiled. The shouts became more muted, then stopped altogether. There was silence. Only the labored breathing coming from the crumpled body.

O'Grady crossed the yard and went to check him.

There was a trickle of blood coming from his thigh. O'Grady took off the hood. The young man seemed to be no more than a teenager. He murmured something. It sounded like "Mum…"

O'Grady rested his arm on the boy's shoulder. With his other hand he pulled out his phone and dialed the emergency services.

The boy shifted and groaned again.

"You'll be OK, son," O'Grady said to him. "But maybe choose your friends more carefully in future."

CHAPTER 5

"WELL, O'GRADY, YOU GOT away with it." The plump man in the navy suit shook him by the hand. "Did you shoot to kill?"

O'Grady shook his head. "I aimed where I meant to aim. I always do."

"The lad's in hospital," the man said. "The police have taken the other two into custody. They're grateful for the arrests."

Philip Tracy, CEO of Headline Security, glanced out of the window at the morning rain, the view across the faceless office blocks with a glimpse of Tower Bridge behind them.

He turned away from the window. "Though the shame is, they'll get away with it. What can the courts give them? They're kids, fourteen, fifteen years old. They'll get a warning, back on the streets in no time. Would have been easier if you'd just shot them all."

O'Grady tensed. "It's not in the job description to take life, Mr. Tracy. Is it?"

"I suppose not." Tracy gave a weak smile. "I just don't like to think of those little gangsters out there, free to strike again. Surely as an ex-cop you feel the same."

O'Grady fixed him with a look. "I'm a security guard, Mr.

Tracy. I'm not working for the law. There was kit to be protected. I protected it. The rights and wrongs of those three boyos, that's not my job."

"But you were a law enforcer, O'Grady."

"That was then."

"So, as a cop—"

"As a cop, I'd have brought those kids to justice. But that was my old life."

"Hmmm." Tracy looked out at the wet streets, the pattering rain. He turned back. "Do you miss it, O'Grady?"

"Well, I think justice is always worth fighting for, Mr. Tracy."

"Would you go back?"

O'Grady picked up his jacket. "I learned a while ago, there are some questions that are best not asked."

"You Irish"—the thin smile again—"all born philosophers," he said.

O'Grady smiled back. "We're called many things," he said. "I've heard worse than that." He turned towards the door. "Will that be all?"

Tracy gave a brief nod. "That will be all. You did well, O'Grady. But maybe best to keep a low profile for a bit. The local coppers aren't too happy about shots being fired. We don't need you for a while—a paid holiday, let's say. Find a nice warm beach for a couple of weeks." He looked out at the rain. "It'll make a change from London."

O'Grady walked out of the reception doors. He stood on the

main road as the buses swished past him, their tires splashing in the gutters.

A holiday, he thought. *When did I last do that? And where would I go? A nice warm beach?*

He imagined himself sitting next to a deep blue sea.

Wherever I go, he thought, *I've still got to take myself with me.*

His phone trilled in his pocket. He snatched it out. Bridie. He clicked to answer.

"Earth," she was saying, her voice shaking.

"What?"

"Earth. The first one. Earth, air, fire and water."

"Bridie, what are you telling me?"

She was shouting now, tearful. "It's started, Finn. Mikey. Found this morning. Killed. By earth."

Her distress cut through the rumble of traffic.

"Mikey?"

"My brother," she said. "He'll come for us all, one by one."

"Bridie, it's a fairy tale—"

"Please believe me. Finn—I don't know who else to ask. Mikey. He was shot, but he was alive when he was buried, the police reckon. That's what I'm saying. Earth. He was found in a newly dug grave, a mask of leaves across his face. It'll be air next, the next one of us to go."

"Bridie—I've had enough of these old Salter tales."

O'Grady watched a cyclist swerve through the traffic in a flash of lime green.

A nice warm beach, Tracy had said.

"Please help us," Bridie was saying. "If not for me, for my little boy…"

Someone else's son. The thoughts rattled through O'Grady's brain. Her brothers, who always despised him, always told Bridie she could do better than the O'Grady clan—wrong side of the valley…

"Once you made me a promise," she said. "A promise made from love. 'If you ever need me,' you said."

And if I don't go, he was thinking, *I'll catch the bus. I'll go back to my flat. I'll sleep for the day, I'll wake this evening. It'll still be London. It'll still be me, alone. And meanwhile…*

"I'm so scared," Bridie said. "So terribly scared. I'm saying it, now. I need you."

I keep my promises, he thought.

"Please," she said. "You can book a flight. I've checked the timings to Dublin airport…."

He listened to her breathing. "OK," he heard himself say. "I'll be there."

CHAPTER 6

O'GRADY LEANED BACK IN his airline seat and sipped at his plastic cup of tea. He looked out at the blue sky, the clouds beneath the wings.

Why am I going back? he asked himself.

There were other questions too. *Why did I leave?*

The answer to that question had always been clear.

Ten years ago, Bridie's little sister Maura was raped and murdered. She was seventeen. O'Grady was a detective sergeant at the time. The *Príomh-Cheannfort,* the Chief Superintendent, was a man called Brian Hawthorne. The case was never brought to court. There were mysterious bungles, evidence left uncollected, DNA samples mislaid, no witnesses found.

Eventually a poor young man pleaded guilty, a haunted, wide-eyed lad who had recently begun a sentence for a killing in a pub brawl. He died in jail, about two years ago now.

O'Grady was persistent. He attempted to chase up the DNA, storing samples where he could. He talked to locals who never quite believed that Betsy's poor lad was capable of such a thing. The boy's friend Aidan had given him an alibi but then retracted it, said he'd been threatened with arrest for illegal hunting; he was told he'd been sighted over on the private grouse moor, though he denied it.

O'Grady didn't give up. With his friend Ryan Fallon, a fellow detective sergeant at the time, they attempted to bring justice for the Salter family. And then came the day when O'Grady found someone who could point to the real killers of Maura Salter. Gregson Elliott. O'Grady arranged to meet him in secret to find out what he knew.

The events of that night were seared into his soul. O'Grady knew Gregson feared for his life. "Don't worry," O'Grady had said. "You're safe with me." He was wrong. Gregson ended up with a bullet through his skull. And O'Grady was given a choice by Brian Hawthorne—to be framed for the murder of Gregson Elliott or leave the force. Hawthorne was powerful, the Chief, the *Priomh-Cheannfort*. Defeated, O'Grady agreed to go. Hawthorne had Fallon sidelined into a rural posting where he found himself investigating the theft of cows and litter problems in the local town. The day he left, Fallon shook O'Grady by the hand. "This is not the end, fella," he'd said. "If you ever need me, call."

Brian Hawthorne was always ruthless. Particularly where his own interests were concerned. O'Grady recalled the smirk on Hawthorne's face as he told him his time as a police officer was over. "I always said you didn't have what it takes, O'Grady. And I was right."

Now, the soft Irish tones of the pilot informed the passengers that the plane would soon be coming in to land in Dublin.

O'Grady thought about sweeping green fields, the soft Irish rain. He thought about home.

He felt only a sense of dread.

CHAPTER 7

O'GRADY WAS GLAD HE'D upgraded his hire car to an Audi A3. The engine purred as he took the bends of the country road. He'd left Dublin and headed west. It was mid-afternoon, with birdsong and sunlight, soft autumnal red and gold across the fields.

He turned off the Galway road, headed north towards Connemara. The countryside became more rugged, the branches of the ancient trees casting shadows across the roads.

A mythical being with a tree for a face. Trying to imagine it amongst the City towers and London buses had been impossible. Now it seemed less preposterous.

He descended the lane towards the town. There was the schoolhouse, closed down now, once ruled by the nuns of the order of St. Joseph. There was the church next door. His childhood home was out of sight, another mile or so across the valley. He wondered who lived there now.

Then he saw the tiled roofs of the Salter farm. His breath quickened as it came into view, a tumbledown grouping of buildings, old barns, a derelict windmill. There was even an ancient waterwheel further down the hill where the river passed through the land.

He parked in the cobbled yard and walked along the track to the house.

The house was beautiful, just as he'd remembered it. A graceful, two-story building, carefully maintained. There was a rose garden. Pots of geraniums made scarlet splashes against the soft gray stone. A column of smoke was issuing from the chimney.

He saw Bridie before she saw him. She was standing with a watering can, tending to her flowers. She wore a pale blue skirt, her auburn hair loosely pinned up, her lithe form unchanged.

He could hardly breathe.

She heard his steps on the stones and looked up. There was a flash of recognition in her green eyes.

"Oh," she breathed, dropping the watering can and stepping towards him. She grasped his sleeve. "Oh, Finn. Thank God you're here."

She led him inside. The warm afternoon sunlight played against the hearth, the wide wooden fireplace. She went to the kitchen range, filled the kettle and placed it on the stove.

Bridie turned and faced him. "Finn—I am so grateful," she said.

He shook his head.

"You can't know how glad I am you're here."

He found his voice. "You...you haven't changed. Not one bit."

"Nor you," she said. "Nor you."

"Where's...?"

"Little Bobby? He's out for a bit, with Vera. He needed some fresh air."

They gazed at each other. "A widow," she said, suddenly. "On my own. After Stuart's death." She fell silent.

The winter before last. The poor man had fallen ill with flu, a lung infection, a rare complication, fatal pneumonia.

"I did hear," O'Grady said. *I thought of calling you,* he was about to add, but then there were heavy steps, a clumping of boots. A large figure stood in the doorway.

"Rick," Bridie said. "My brother. You remember Finn—"

The man was thickset, red-faced, with thin gingery hair and a stubbly chin. He slumped down into a chair at the table.

Bridie placed a mug of tea in front of him.

He took a slurp of it. "I remember O'Grady all right," he said.

"He's come to help." Her voice was tight. She stood over her brother, one hand on her hip.

He pushed the mug towards her across the old oak table. "Sugar," he said.

Bridie stirred two spoons of sugar into her brother's tea.

O'Grady wondered how these boys had come from their parents. Their mother, Ellen, had been a graceful woman with a lively smile and a caring soul. The father, Richard Salter, had been a clever, bookish man. He'd started researching local history, working on Irish music and folk singing. It was he who'd taken up the Green Man idea. It had been mentioned from time to time by some of the old farmers. Richard never felt that he had a right to the land, and a kind of guilt had always haunted the family. This was made worse by the death of his wife from cancer, two months short of her sixtieth birthday.

Bridie poured tea for O'Grady. They settled at the table.

Rick fixed O'Grady with a glowering look. "So," he said. "My brother's body is in the Garda fridge. And you're here to save us. Much good that will do."

"That's enough." Bridie's voice was sharp.

"Who's next?" Rick went on, ignoring his sister. "That's what I want to know."

"The old story," she said. "It could be any of us."

"The story." He gave a sneer. "Old James Salter, our grand-dad, took this scrub patch of land that no one else wanted and made a good farm and a working mill. The locals would never accept it. He was a clever man, that's all. He made a living, a good living. And for some reason, our father chose to feel guilty, to carry a fool's belief in ghosts."

O'Grady stared at the teapot, the dark brown china peeping out from the knitted tea cozy with its stripes of blue and cream.

It was familiar, this leaching resentment. All to do with family inheritance. Richard had settled the farm and house on his daughter, sidestepping the traditional path that would have given it all to Rick, who had had to settle for a modern three-bedroomed semi on the edge of the town.

Rick interrupted his thoughts. "If ghosts are to blame, maybe they're hiding out in the ghost estate," he said, mockingly.

O'Grady looked up. "What estate?"

Rick tilted his head towards the window. "Out there. The other side of our farm."

"There's a ghost estate there?" O'Grady said.

Rick nodded. "You remember it. Brand-new housing, built in the boom times. And then they couldn't sell it. Like all these boom-time developments. Ghost estates. Fairy estates. They're all over the region."

"But now the one across the way there has been bought up by a local company," Bridie said. "They're developing it again."

"Luxury homes," Rick said. "They reckon there'll be money. Rolling lawns. Golf courses, everything—"

His words were cut short by a rush of feet and the sound of laughter. A little boy tumbled into the room and ran to his mother. He had thick dark curls of hair, soft brown eyes and was wearing a red hand-knitted sweater.

For the first time Bridie smiled. She scooped her son up onto her lap and held him close.

An elderly lady had appeared behind him, with a lined face, neat gray hair and a warm smile. "He wanted to see the visitor," she said.

"Vera, you remember Finn O'Grady," Bridie said.

O'Grady got to his feet. "Miss Joyce. Pleasure to see you again."

She smiled. "Of course I remember you," she said. Her eyes were on him, her hand held out. She wore a long tweed skirt and lace-up boots.

"You'll know Vera used to teach at the old charity school here," Bridie said. "Before she joined us."

O'Grady shook her hand.

"A Garda, you were," she said. "When did you leave us? Three, four years ago now?"

"Three and a half years," he said.

She shook her head. "Ach," she said. "One of the few honest ones. No wonder there was no room for you." Her eyes were still fixed on him. "Shame they let you go," she said.

"And you worked with Mr. Salter," O'Grady said, remembering, as Vera sat down at the table. "Richard Salter," he added.

Vera nodded.

"She helped him with his editing," Bridie said. "His folk-song research. He always said he could never have written his books without you."

Vera gave a smile, a dip of her head. Bobby jumped down from his mother's lap and went to her, taking hold of her hand. "Nana Vee," he said. "I want a biscuit."

Vera laughed.

Rick stirred from his place. "At least Nana Vee has the sense not to believe in ghosts," he said.

Vera flashed him a look. "It's not that," she said. "All I said was that whoever's done this has got it wrong. The Green Man tale is about redemption. He comes back from the dead. Like the seeds sown in the fields, that rise up to be the wheat. In the old songs, he's no killer. He's the life force, the opposite of death."

Rick got to his feet with a scrape of his chair. "Well, whatever it is, man or ghost, it's got to be stopped. If you're here to save us, O'Grady, you'd better start now."

O'Grady stood to face Rick. "Sure," he said. "I know where I want to start. Let's go and see this ghost estate."

CHAPTER 8

THEY WALKED UP THE hill, away from the farm, Rick striding ahead towards the new housing, Bridie and O'Grady side by side, slightly behind. The afternoon sun flickered through the trees behind them. O'Grady was struck by the barren land, the flattened plain before them. He could see pristine buildings, facades of brand-new brick, lifeless windows staring blankly out across the dried, cracked mud.

"Who's the development company?" O'Grady asked.

"Quite a complex set-up," Rick began.

"There's a group of company directors," Bridie said. "My husband's brother is involved." She turned to O'Grady. "You remember Sean? He made a lot of money from the bookmakers—"

"Sean O'Connor fixed the machines," Rick interrupted. "Took easy money from brainless punters."

"He's in property now," Bridie went on. "We don't see much of him."

"That's where the golf course will be," Rick said, waving his arm towards the expanse of clay. "My son Jason is working for them too."

"A family business, then?" O'Grady glanced at him, but he

didn't reply. O'Grady looked at the strangely parched earth. "They'll need water for a golf course," he said. "And this land has always been dry."

"They'll get it," Rick replied. "The old stream flows down the hill from here. But there's all sorts of technology these days. Pumps and that."

"Dad." The voice came from behind them. O'Grady turned to see a tall, sauntering young man in tight jeans and designer boots.

"Jason," Rick said. "You remember Finn O'Grady."

The young man frowned at him.

"This is Jason, my son," Rick said.

"Ah." O'Grady offered his hand, which the young man took with some reluctance. "So, you're working on the site?"

Jason nodded, eyeing O'Grady from under his blond fringe, unsmiling.

"With Sean O'Connor," O'Grady said.

The boy nodded again.

"And who else?"

"What do you mean?" Jason said.

"The other directors of the company," O'Grady said. "I gather there are several."

Jason glanced up at Rick. "Apart from Sean? There's a guy who does the money, over in Dublin. Alastair something he's called. And there's another guy called Kiley MacAteer."

O'Grady froze. "Kiley MacAteer," he repeated. He looked across at Bridie. She looked at the ground. "Now we're getting somewhere."

CHAPTER 9

O'GRADY WALKED AHEAD, WITH Bridie a few steps behind him. They'd left Jason with his father surveying the site, Jason pointing out where work was about to start again, finishing the roofs, planting hedges and lawns.

O'Grady stopped, waited for Bridie. She was drooping and sullen. She looked up at him. "I knew it," she said.

"Knew what?"

The last rays of the sun caught the red of her hair. "I should never have asked you back." She was level with him now, her eyes fiery and defiant.

"What are you implying?"

"Your history with Hawthorne will always obscure your view of the truth. It did before, and it is now."

"I don't need to tell you about the friendship between Kiley MacAteer and Brian Hawthorne."

She walked away, striding down the hill to where the fields turned green again, to where the Salter farmhouse nestled between the hedgerows.

O'Grady watched her go. *If only you knew,* he wanted to say to her.

He'd known Hawthorne since schooldays. When they were both just small boys at St. Joseph's school, where the nuns ruled the children's lives.

Little Brian Hawthorne was round and pink-faced, and seemed to know how to pretend to be good. The nuns adored him. But O'Grady always seemed to get on the wrong side of them. The sisters would stand little Finn on a chair, to give him time to "contemplate his sins," as they would say. His legs aching, he would watch the sisters glide past in their steel-gray habits, while Brian would mock him behind their backs. The boys would often come to blows, resulting in more standing on chairs for O'Grady, more sneering triumph for Hawthorne. Once, in a particularly vicious fight, O'Grady threw a powerful right hook which caught his enemy under his left eye. Hawthorne still had the scar.

O'Grady walked slowly back towards the farm. Bridie had already reached the house. He took a detour, went through the iron gates at the entrance to the track. He wandered around the tumbledown barns, thinking about James Salter and his English certainties, his sense of having a right to this Irish land. O'Grady thought about how those certainties had not passed down to James's melancholic, academic son. Now Richard had left behind a fearful daughter shadowed by the unresolved violent death of her sister. Only the boys seemed to have escaped Richard's inherent guilt, with Rick carrying the same swaggering entitlement of his grandfather, and now passing that on to his own son.

O'Grady found himself standing by the old derelict windmill. He watched the skeletal sails circle slowly in the dusk, round and round. He thought about their former purpose, milling the grain to feed the people. Now, all meaning had deserted them. They turned uselessly.

In the gusts of wind through the sails, O'Grady heard a whisper of a name. Kiley MacAteer.

I know what I have to do, he thought.

CHAPTER 10

O'GRADY'S AUDI SCREECHED TO a halt outside the Garda HQ in town. The town clock said two minutes to eleven. He was aware of waiting for something, then remembered how the clock tower would strike the hour, a familiar dull tolling.

That morning he'd sat at the kitchen table, watching Bobby eat breakfast cereal with one hand and push his blue toy car along the table's edge with the other.

Bridie had barely spoken.

The night before she'd made up a bed for him in the downstairs study, a fold-down single bed with old Irish linen sheets and a patchwork quilt.

Vera had gone home, back to her cozy cottage and her two tabby cats. She'd hesitated, her hand on Bridie's shoulder. "You'll be all right, will you?" she'd said, looking uncertainly at O'Grady. Then she'd given Bobby a hug and walked off into the night.

Bridie had cooked for the three of them, baked cod with potatoes and apple crumble to follow. O'Grady had picked up Bobby's teddy and talked for him in a funny voice. Bobby had laughed and O'Grady had looked at the warm fire, at Bridie's illuminated smile, and had laughed too.

Later Bridie had put Bobby to bed. O'Grady had heard her singing to him, a Gaelic lullaby:

"Seoithín, seo hó, mo stór é, mo leanbh…"

"Hush-a-bye, baby, my darling, my child…."

He remembered previous times when she had been working on her father's folk songs and he'd hear her clear, sweet voice telling stories of love and desire, of warriors and exile.

Now he stood under the town clock tower in the busy street and listened to the bells strike the hour. He slammed the door of his car and walked towards the Garda HQ, an imposing, white stone building.

He strode up the steps.

He stood in reception. He'd dressed carefully. Crisp blue jeans, his black leather jacket, expensive shoes.

"I'm here to see the *Príomh-Cheannfort,*" he said.

The young woman on reception had a neat black fringe, pouting red lips, and was wearing a white blouse draped over generous curves. "Do you have an appointment?"

"Tell him O'Grady's here," he said.

She fixed him with her dark gaze. "You need an appointment," she said.

He looked at her name badge.

"You're wrong there, Miss Riley," he said.

She smiled at him, and he felt as if he'd passed a test. "I'm afraid I'm right," she said, but she was blushing now.

He smiled back. "Don't worry. I've known him since we were small boys at St. Joseph's."

He strode away. He could feel her eyes still fixed on him.

The corridor was familiar, the staircases with their wide stone steps, the sweeping banisters.

He reached the first floor, walked along the green-carpeted corridor and stopped in front of an old oak door.

He knocked, then turned the handle. The door swung open.

Chief Superintendent Hawthorne was sitting at his desk. He seemed more jowly than O'Grady remembered, more red-faced, more overfed. His collar was off-white and tight at the neck. His jacket was a shiny navy, stretched over his belly. He had strands of gray hair combed across his head.

His small pale eyes focused on O'Grady. Then came recognition.

"What the fuck are you doing here?"

O'Grady stood in front of his desk. "Your friend is building on the land next door to the Salters."

Hawthorne gathered himself, composed his face into the familiar sneer. "And what is that to me, O'Grady?"

"Kiley MacAteer," O'Grady said. "Still causing trouble."

"People here can do as they please without interference from jumped-up ex-guards." The emphasis was on the "ex." "I never expected to see you again, O'Grady."

"I want answers, Hawthorne."

Hawthorne's eyes narrowed. "I'm warning you, O'Grady. I don't know what's brought you back to Ireland, but if I were you, I'd get the next plane out of here. I got rid of you once. I can do it again."

"Sure, Hawthorne. You got rid of me once. Once is enough." He turned and walked out, leaving the door wide open behind him.

He headed for the staircase. Two men were walking towards him along the corridor. He recognized them. One was Sean O'Connor, brother of Bridie's husband Stuart. With him was a large thickset man with neat dark hair graying at the temples, and wearing an expensive-looking suit.

Kiley MacAteer.

There was a flash of acknowledgement from MacAteer, a look in his eyes. It was a hard, triumphant look. O'Grady clenched his hands into fists.

It's over, MacAteer, he wanted to say, as their eyes locked. Instead, he stepped to one side and walked on.

There will be a time for that, he thought to himself, as he reached the stairs. *There will be a time for justice.*

CHAPTER 11

"SO, IT GOT YOU nowhere." Bridie O'Connor stood in her living room in the dusky evening light. She smoothed a linen cloth across the dining table. "I could have told you that. Going into town, annoying Hawthorne, stirring things up."

She crossed the room, switched on some lights and went into the kitchen.

"I saw Kiley MacAteer," he said. "Walking along the corridor with Sean, your brother-in-law."

She reappeared with two plates which she placed on the table: perfectly cooked lamb chops, steamed potatoes, redcurrant sauce. She sat down opposite him.

He picked up his wine glass. "Kiley MacAteer," he repeated.

Her eyes flashed with anger. "And what's that to me? I'm here with my brother dead, with my son threatened." She looked at him. "Finn, I called on you in the hope that you would understand. I was clearly wrong." Her eyes welled with tears. "Instead of listening to what I was telling you, you've got caught up in your old fights, old battles and grudges." She dashed at her eyes with the back of her hand. "I should have remembered what you were really like, Finn. Why you and me came to an end.

I should have remembered those times. Not the times before."
She was staring at the tablecloth, tracing a finger around a patch
of stitching.

Her words were like a slap. O'Grady put down his glass. He
leaned across to her and touched her hand. "I'm sorry, Bridie."

She looked up at him, gave a shrug.

"So," he said. "Tell me. Tell me again. And I promise I'll
listen."

She circled the wine in her glass.

"Your sister," he prompted. "Maura. All those years ago…"

She sighed, her plate untouched. She began to speak. "She'd
talk about him, in those months before she died. The Green
Man. She'd go on about our family guilt, the way our grandfather behaved, stealing the land. Maura would read all our
father's old books. She was haunted by it. She'd say our grandfather had done a terrible wrong, and that the Green Man would
come to claim what was his own."

"And then she died. A brutal death."

"My father blamed himself. He said he should have listened.
She knew she was in danger. No one protected her.…" She
clapped her hand over her mouth, shook her head.

"She was attacked by real men," O'Grady said. "Not ghosts.
And they were never brought to justice. Kiley MacAteer—"

Her hand went up. "I don't want to hear that name."

"Never brought to justice, despite all my best efforts," he
went on. "And now lording it around the land next door."

She breathed out.

"And you've had to live with that injustice all this time," he said.

She shook her head. "I've just found a way of managing it, that's all. It's the same as when Stuart died." She lifted her head. "We Salters are cursed. I'm cursed."

They sat in silence, each with their thoughts. Bridie spoke again. "I always knew he'd come. Mikey was killed by earth. It'll be air next. Someone will die by air."

O'Grady watched her. She seemed more beautiful than ever, her skin illuminated by the flicker of the fire, her hair in soft curls under the low light. He thought of this house, of Richard Salter taking refuge in his work, and now his daughter feeling she too must bury herself in the old stories.

He tried again. "Bridie—your grandfather wasn't a nice man. He was a bully. He was hated in the town. What if…what if this isn't a ghost? What if there's some real bad feeling that's never gone away?"

A flash of rage. "Why do you need one or the other? I'm not saying that my grandfather wasn't a difficult man. But why can't you hear what I'm telling you? If Stuart was here—" She stopped, but it was too late.

"If Stuart was here, you'd never have called on me," O'Grady said. "Is that what you mean?"

Bridie's eyes were fixed on his, dark with feeling. She tried to speak, but shook her head.

In the silence they remembered. How he'd promised to look after her forever. How he'd talked of their future, of the house they'd live in. He'd even started to build it. He'd bought a plot of land further along the valley, laid the concrete base, put up half a brick wall…

Maura's death, and the circumstances surrounding it, ate away at their relationship. He'd become obsessed with finding out the truth, just as Bridie had retreated into fear and grief. His days had been taken up with endless fruitless attempts to gather evidence; his evening hours were spent in Tynan's bar.

He remembered how Bridie had despaired of him. How Stuart O'Connor, dependable Stuart, the local carpenter, had come to her rescue. How O'Grady, realizing that he'd lost the only two things that mattered to him, his woman and his job, had seen that he had to go.

O'Grady got to his feet. "I'm going to bed," he said. In the doorway he turned. "Bridie—I give you my word. I will do my best to protect you and your family from whatever this threat is. I will fight to keep you safe. But please remember this. You and I, we both made promises. I learned long ago not to hold you to yours. You called me, and I came to you. That's all I can offer you now."

He turned away, went into the darkness of the hallway. She heard the study door slam shut.

The hammering on his door, when it came much later that night, woke him from deep sleep. Bridie was there, in a white nightdress, screaming his name, her phone clutched in one hand. "Finn—now, quick, come on!" She was grabbing at his arm, pulling him towards the door.

"What—?"

"Air," she was shouting. "They called me. The windmill—" They were outside in the damp black night. "It's happened again."

CHAPTER 12

THERE WAS NO MOON. The Audi headlights cut beams through the mist. He drove fast up the track, Bridie silent and shivering at his side.

They rounded the corner. The mill was a towering shadow, a black silhouette against the sky. The sails were turning, slowly. There seemed to be something attached to them.

They jumped from the car, running close, seeing, as they got near, a human form tied to the blades, turning, round and round. Limp. Lifeless.

"Rick!" Bridie screamed. "Rick…"

The corpse circled. The branches of the trees were ghost-white in the headlight beams. Locals had appeared, gathering in silent groups, staring blankly up at the dead body of Rick Salter.

CHAPTER 13

THERE WERE POLICE, AMBULANCES. Bridie had called Vera, who had gone to the house to sit with Bobby. "Fast asleep, bless him," Vera had reported. "Managed not to wake at all."

O'Grady went to find the police. There were two young men, one black, one white, standing at the foot of the mill.

"Detective Sergeant Driscoll," the first Garda said. "And this is DC Laverty." DC Laverty was pale-haired and hunched with cold.

All three men gazed up at the sails.

"What do you make of it?" O'Grady asked.

"He'd been shot," Driscoll said. "Seems to be a fatal wound, from behind. Shot in the back of the head. But for some reason they took him, dead, dying maybe, and strung him up here, and then set the motor to turn—on a night like this, no wind, the air still." He stared upwards. "They seemed to have wanted theatre as well as a killing."

O'Grady smiled, in spite of the circumstances. "Thanks for your help," he said.

"You with the lady?" the young sergeant said.

He gave a nod. "I used to be a Garda," he heard himself say to them. "A *sáirsint* too."

Now, as the dawn began to touch the sky with gray, he went to stand with Bridie. They watched as the emergency crews stilled the windmill, climbed the tower, cut the ropes which held the body, carried him back down, laid him on a stretcher. There was a pause, a silence, in those moments before the birds began to sing. Then they laid a cloth over him and covered his face.

Bridie began to sob, loud gasps of grief. She ran to her brother, pulled back the cloth, flung herself across the body. O'Grady was at her side, crouched beside her. After long minutes her sobbing abated. He put his arm around her and helped her to her feet. She leaned in to him as he walked her away, back to the car.

He drove her back to her house. She was white-faced with cold, with grief. He helped her indoors, sat her at the table, draped a blanket around her shoulders and lit the fire.

After he'd boiled a kettle he placed a mug of tea in front of her.

She stared vacantly at the rising steam.

He sat opposite her. "I'm sorry," he said.

She raised her eyes to his.

"All that time we were sitting here arguing about ghosts," he began, "and your brother's life was on the line. That's what you're thinking, isn't it?"

She gathered the blanket around her.

"Someone sought him out, tracked him down, shot him

dead," O'Grady went on. "There was a fatal shotgun wound, from behind. He didn't stand a chance."

"Air." She spoke at last, her voice thin. "Whoever did this knows the old rhyme, the old stories."

"Bridie—whoever did this wanted Rick Salter dead."

She stared at the table.

"Your brother was lording it around the new estate," O'Grady said. "Thinking he owned the place. Like the old Salters. And someone was angry."

She said nothing, so he went on. "I can only work from what's in front of me. So, let's start with your Green Man story. This account that you've been giving me, the old rhyme. Earth, then air...so, fire next?"

She looked up at him, nodded.

"Bridie—let's say there's a threat to your family, we can agree on that. And let's say that I will do everything I can to keep you safe. Is that a deal?"

She gave another small nod. She got to her feet, wrapped the blanket around her and left the room. He heard her feet on the stairs, going up to her bed.

CHAPTER 14

HE WENT TO HIS little room and lay down on the bed. The gray light of the early morning crept in through the study curtains. Bobby seemed to be still sleeping. Vera too was asleep, in the guest room upstairs. Bridie had gone to bed but O'Grady imagined her lying, shocked and afraid, her eyes wide open.

He wished he could help her. He wished he could reach her.

He heard a distant church clock strike the hour. Seven o'clock.

He wouldn't go back to sleep now.

In his mind, he saw the towering windmill blades, their slow turning, the bleeding body of Rick Salter roped across them, turning too.

It takes more than a leaf-masked ghost to carry out a shooting at point-blank range.

O'Grady's thoughts took him back to the day before, the corridors of Garda HQ, Hawthorne's sneering face, the tight-faced hostility of Kiley MacAteer.

He remembered how MacAteer used to be when he was young. Good-looking, dark-eyed, he played football for the local team and worked as the manager of a chain of sportswear shops. Always there with a joke, always good for a laugh. He got promoted, made some money, drove nice cars. And that was when he started dating Maura Salter.

Maura was sixteen, with the Salter good looks. Darker-haired than her big sister Bridie, but she had the same soft grace. She was considered a catch, and Kiley would brag about it in pubs, how he'd got the prettiest girl in town, how when he married her he'd have the Salter farm too.

And then, aged seventeen, she broke it off. Told him she didn't want to see him anymore. Her family breathed a sigh of relief. Kiley MacAteer was known to be a bully, known to be someone who was used to getting his own way. While she was with him, Maura had become cowed and shy. But once she'd declared the relationship over, she'd become taller, somehow, with brighter clothes and the odd slick of lipstick. She'd begun to spend time with a young American, Gregson Elliott, a researcher who'd come from Yale to work with Richard Salter on Irish folk tales, in particular on the myths that had traveled to the States in the wake of the Irish potato famine in the 1840s. He said he'd always felt like an Irishman: "My mother was a Murphy, though it turns out that's true for about half of all Americans." Charming, good-looking, sandy-haired, with old-fashioned good manners, he'd settled into the town. When asked if he ever missed his life back home he would express relief to be away from his large family, "far too many brothers, cousins, godparents—and the beer's better here too."

For a few months, Maura seemed happier. The family seemed

happier. Richard relaxed in the knowledge that his younger daughter was safe from the bullying MacAteer and in the much more kindred company of Gregson. Gregson became part of the family. He got on well with everyone. He even joined Sean in his roofing business. "Makes a change from old books," he'd said, "to be up a roof with a hammer." Sean would tease him, call him Murphy. Bridie was pleased that her brother-in-law had a friend, as Sean had always had a reputation for being difficult and too quick with his fists.

But then, Maura began to have her terrors. She'd talk about the Green Man and how he would wreak his revenge. Vera and Gregson would try to explain that the Green Man myth couldn't possibly be used to threaten harm in this way, but she would turn away from them, locked in her own versions of the story. All through the autumn she would be found wandering near the watermill, murmuring the old songs. And then, the following March, St. Patrick's Day itself, she was found in a ditch, strangled to death, having been raped.

It was a big case locally. Brian Hawthorne, recently promoted, took it on. O'Grady, as a sergeant, was part of the investigation. "So," Hawthorne had said, "let's talk to her boyfriend. It's always the last person to see the victim alive."

Gregson was shaky, nervous. He'd been due to meet her, he said. "I waited and waited. She never turned up."

"And where were you before that?" O'Grady asked him.

"I was working. With Sean. We had a building job that day. Honest. Ask him. It's the truth, I promise you...."

"Yeah," Sean had said, when questioned. "We were working on a barn conversion, over in Polkeen. Old Murphy was whistling away, checking the time, saying he was due to meet Maura later that evening, they'd raise a glass to the holy Saint himself while they were about it.…As far as I knew, he went off to meet her."

Gregson was questioned again. "She never arrived. Honest to God. I stood there, by the old bus stop, opposite the post office—we always met there. No sign of her. I tried her phone. After an hour I ran to the farm, raised the alarm. And then it was the next day.…"

The next day, in a cold gray dawn, she was found in a ditch, by the side of the main Galway road. Half stripped, her broken, clay-white body seared with the brutal markings of a violent end.

Gregson blamed himself. "I should have looked for her," he'd say. He'd talk to O'Grady, ask if there was any news. O'Grady would say no, no news so far, we're still gathering evidence, please don't blame yourself, Gregson, what could you have done differently…?

And then one day Hawthorne announced, with regret, that the trail had gone cold.

O'Grady would say to his boss, "I have some questions on the Salter case. How well do you know Kiley MacAteer? Where was Mr. MacAteer the night that Maura Salter was assaulted and killed?"

At first, Chief Superintendent Hawthorne entertained these questions, pretended to go along with his keenness to pursue the case. He'd also answer questions from journalists: "We're working on the evidence; my *sáirsint* here is gathering clues, we won't give up…."

After a while, Hawthorne tired of the questions.

The poor lad blamed was Ivor O'Dowd, a hapless youth with a father who'd run away to sea and a dubious livelihood breeding fighting dogs. He'd got embroiled in a fight outside a dockside pub in town and had recently been jailed for assault. Hawthorne's team insisted that circumstantial evidence placed him within some miles of the Salter farm the night of Maura's death. He was interrogated for twenty-four hours. His bruises were still visible when he was dragged to court and pleaded guilty.

For the Salter household, the death of Maura brought changes. Gregson Elliott lost his enthusiasm for his work. Richard, too, retreated into grief, into silence, into despair. Vera would cook meals that she knew he liked, only to see them left untouched. She would try to get him to visit the doctor, but he would take no notice. Even when his breathing shortened, when he grew thin and tired, and she would tell anyone who'd listen that there was something the matter: "The poor man is ill, I can tell heartbreak when I see it…." But he was beyond help.

Richard Salter was found dead in his bed on St. Patrick's Day, two years to the day after his daughter met her terrible fate. At his funeral, Vera stood straight-backed and dry-eyed. She was dressed all in black, a long, belted dress with a high collar. She left the church as the organist played the final piece of music, a chorale prelude by Bach, walking out before the congregation. In the aftermath of her sister's and then her father's deaths, Bridie wilted and drooped, burdened by a kind of survivor's guilt. The Salter boys brazened it out, hardened their hearts. Bridie took on her father's pain, his sense of responsibility. The Green Man began to haunt her as it had her sister.

As O'Grady lay in his narrow bed, the same unanswered questions that had plagued him years ago still plagued him now.

CHAPTER 15

THE HOUSE WAS STILL silent. O'Grady got up and dressed. He left the house and walked out of the lane, up the hill, towards the ghost estate.

The site was deserted. A thin breeze wafted here and there through the empty windows. O'Grady looked back across the valley, to the lush green fields of the Salter farm. The trees bent and creaked in the wind. He thought about the Green Man, emerging from their branches, striding up the hill to wreak revenge.

O'Grady heard footsteps behind him. He turned to see a figure crossing the rough stone path.

Jason Salter.

O'Grady approached him.

Jason seemed jumpy, nervy and hostile. "Come to gloat, have you, O'Grady? I saw you at the windmill last night."

"No, lad." O'Grady spoke gently. "I've come to tell you to get out of here."

Jason's face tightened. "Not you as well, with this Green Man rubbish."

"Your father—"

"The police are on the case. There's nothing you can add, O'Grady."

"Jason—what happened last night—"

Jason was shouting now. "That's enough, O'Grady. You haven't had to see your dad like that, like…I saw him in the morgue, afterwards. I've never seen a dead body before.…"

He crumpled suddenly, sat heavily on the ground. O'Grady went to his side. "Jason," he said. "Bridie's right. There's a danger to the Salters. You need to get away from this site."

Jason turned to him. "I'm not having you planting those thoughts in my mind. That's what my dad said. You coming back here, allowing poor Bridie to go on about ghosts, allowing her to think you care." He stumbled to his feet, a spot of red on each cheek, his bluster returned. "They're paying me well here," he said. "Sean and the others."

O'Grady had stood up too and faced him. "If you think those people employing you are on your side, you're wrong. They're using you, Jason. You're a Salter. They need you for their plan to take the farmland. You're in danger, boy."

Jason threw him a harsh smile. "Just like my dad said. You're spending too long with Auntie Bridie and her ghosts."

O'Grady grabbed Jason's arm. "Look, boy. Look." With his other arm he waved towards the estate. "This is going to be a golf course? How can they do that without water? But if you look at the lie of the land…" He pointed the other way, towards the river, the old red bricks of the watermill, the green fields beyond, dotted with grazing sheep. "If they can get the

Salter land they can pump all the water they like from the mill race."

Jason wriggled from O'Grady's grip and faced him. "So, you're saying Sean O'Connor is going to get the Green Man to finish me off so he can get hold of the farm?"

"I'm trying to warn you," O'Grady said. "Your father suffered a terrible fate last night. Why do you think that happened?"

Jason had his hands on his hips. "The police are on the case, O'Grady."

"The police? The police couldn't catch the true killers of Maura Salter."

Jason gave a half-smile. "We've heard all this before, O'Grady. You're a failed Garda. Doesn't mean the rest of us can't trust them."

"And who said that to you? Kiley MacAteer?"

Jason didn't answer, but his face hardened.

"I promised Bridie I'd try to warn you. I've done what I can." O'Grady turned away and walked back to the farm, leaving Jason standing there, a solitary figure on the bare land.

CHAPTER 16

"I'VE TALKED TO JASON," O'Grady said as he walked back into the farmhouse. Bridie was sitting at the table. She was dressed now, in jeans and a loose jumper with pastel stripes.

"Did he listen?"

O'Grady shook his head.

"I expect he went on about poor Auntie Bridie and her ghosts. I expect you both did."

He met her eyes. "The lad has just seen his dad killed. He was in no fit state to listen."

She picked up her mug of tea, stared into it. "It'll be fire next," she said.

"Bridie—you know what I think. It suits these men, the old myth. They're using it as a cover."

She breathed out, a weary sigh. She looked up him. "Finn— I'm not asking you to believe in ghosts. I'm asking you to believe in me."

He was about to answer, but there was a rush of small feet. "Nana Vee says she'll take me to the cogs today." Bobby came running into the room. "And she says I'm not to be scared of the Green Man. She says he doesn't mean anyone any harm. We're going to the cogs today. Can I go, Mammy? Say I can go." He climbed onto her lap and put his little hands on either side of her face.

Bridie smiled. "It's the old waterwheel. It's your favorite thing, Bobby boy, isn't it, watching the cogs. Of course you can go." He climbed off her lap and ran outside.

She turned to O'Grady. "Bobby can turn the handle and make the gears work. He loves it. Vera takes him for a treat."

"He's a brave boy," O'Grady said. "Like his mother." He gazed down at her, and she looked up at him. He wanted to take her in his arms. But she stood and went to wash up.

Later that morning, O'Grady wandered around the Salter estate. He found himself at the old watermill. It was a one-story building made of red bricks in an ornate crisscross pattern. There was a rhythmic, metallic sound coming from inside. He bent to go through the low door.

In the dim light he could see two figures. Little Bobby was turning a handle, staring fascinated at the mechanism. The cog-wheels turned, now disconnected from the main wheel, but still clicking round, all interleaved. Vera stood at his side, watching the wheels too.

She turned, greeted O'Grady with a smile. He stood with them in their rapt silence. The cogs turned, clicked. Outside, the huge waterwheel hung over the weir, jerking to and fro in the water's rush.

O'Grady tired of it before Bobby did. He wandered away,

along the canal path, treading through the autumn leaves. He knew where he was headed.

There was a break in the trees, a lane turning away from the river's edge. He walked along the lane. A fence, a gate. And there it was, the half-built house. He could see the brick walls, the joists of the roof open to the sky.

He pushed at the gate. The concrete floor was covered with leaves and pigeon feathers.

My dream home. He looked around. Every brick that we laid, me and Ryan Fallon, was supposed to be a step towards my new life.

Not this. Not this empty ruin.

The dream died. Or rather, it was killed. By Brian Hawthorne.

He stared at the floor. Trying not to remember.

Gregson Elliott. Shot dead. And all because I asked him for the truth.

And now the thoughts crowded in, the memories.

After Maura's death, Gregson stayed around, trying to help Richard, trying to keep their work going. But Richard shrank into melancholy as his life lost meaning. After Richard's death, Gregson too lost interest in the old books. He retreated into silence, taking refuge in the building work with Sean. When asked, he'd say something about hammering being therapeutic: "It helps, you know, rhythmic, physical work…"

O'Grady would often get the sense that he had more to say. Some evenings, as they sat side by side in Tynan's bar, Gregson would turn to him over his pint of stout, as if about to speak, then turn away and shake his head.

One day, O'Grady came upon Gregson packing his bags, in the converted barn that he'd made his home.

"What are you doing, Elliott?" he asked.

"Back to the States," Gregson mumbled, throwing shirts into a zip-up case. "Family things…"

"A bit sudden, isn't it?"

Gregson wouldn't meet his eyes. "My aunt," he said. "Getting on a bit…losing her mind…"

O'Grady didn't bother to ask any further. *Why?* he'd thought. *Why should you go all the way back to Connecticut because of an aunt when there are all those cousins, siblings and godchildren to look after her?*

The reason he didn't ask was the look of fear on Gregson's face. O'Grady had seen that expression before. The look of a man fleeing for his life.

"Tell me what you know," O'Grady said, even though Gregson was standing there, shaking his head.

"Hawthorne. And his thugs. Hawthorne knows what you know. He knows you could start up the whole Salter case again—"

Gregson put his hand across O'Grady's mouth.

"We'll go somewhere safe," O'Grady offered after pulling away Gregson's hand.

"There's nowhere safe," Gregson replied.

"My house. It's a building site. No one goes there—it's out in the woods."

Gregson hesitated, and O'Grady saw his honest good nature winning out, his belief that justice should be done.

"Tonight," Gregson agreed. But his voice was tight with fear.

So that evening, O'Grady set out along the lane. It was warm for March; the sun had just set. He was thinking about his new home, how he'd started the joists for the roof; soon there'd be a time when the bare brick walls would be painted, the concrete base would have polished oak floors, there would be a roof, fireplaces, warmth…

Gregson had got there before him. He was lying, shot dead, on the makeshift floor. His body was still warm. The blood from the single wound to the side of his head made a widening puddle on the smooth white ground.

O'Grady had looked down at the body of his friend. Gregson's eyes were wide open, the same good-natured, boyish look, even in death.

And all because I asked him to meet me.

Then, shouting, hands upon him, rough, male hands, rough voices, Gaelic insults. O'Grady's arms were twisted behind him, his head locked into a thick, stinking elbow. Trying, helplessly, to wrench himself free.

Hawthorne's thugs. The Devlin boys—he'd know those voices anywhere. The twins, Stig and Dooley, known for their brutality and their background as amateur boxers.

And then another voice.

"Keep him in one piece, lads."

Hawthorne's voice. Hawthorne's face, looming over him.

"Oh dear, oh dear, O'Grady. What have we here?"

O'Grady had looked up into the small pink eyes.

"A murder weapon?" Hawthorne had picked up a pistol from the ground. Hawthorne was wearing blue forensic latex gloves. He held the Ruger under O'Grady's nose.

"This must be what you used to shoot the poor bugger," Hawthorne went on.

"You won't find my prints on that," O'Grady had said, through lips half crushed by a tattooed forearm.

Hawthorne had laughed. "Fingerprints? You're talking to the Chief Super, O'Grady. The *Príomh-Cheannfort*. What do I need with fingerprints? That's for the little guys, the form-fillers, the fact-checkers." He'd turned on his heel. "Stig, Dooley. Take him away. But I don't want a mark on him—is that understood?"

O'Grady had been bundled into a windowless van. He'd been handcuffed. One of the Devlin boys had occasionally landed a punch to his ribs—"Just to make sure you behave for the boss," they'd said.

He'd been thrown in a police cell. The next day, he'd been marched up to Hawthorne's office.

Hawthorne had leaned back in his chair and surveyed him. "I hope they looked after you," he'd said. "I gather the breakfasts downstairs are every bit the equal of the Gresham." He'd laughed. O'Grady had stood tall, staring straight ahead.

"Well, O'Grady." He'd put his hands to his waistcoat pockets. "It seems to me you've got a choice. You can walk out of here and promise you'll never bother me again. Or you can be charged with the murder of Gregson Elliott. But I can't imagine either of us wants to go through all that, do we?"

O'Grady was silent.

"What I think is, it doesn't suit you being a Garda. Too many questions to ask. Too many unsolved mysteries. So I put it to you that it's time you stopped. Stopped being an officer. Stopped asking questions. And in return, I'll leave you alone. And I'll tell these cute twins to leave you alone too."

Stig and Dooley Devlin had appeared in the doorway. They were in identical baggy vest tops, both rubbing their tattooed forearms, up and down, in a gesture of anticipation.

"Take him away," Hawthorne had said.

The Devlin boys had walked him down the stairs to the front door. He'd been half walked, half thrown onto the steps outside.

Ryan Fallon had been approaching the main door. "Finn— what the fuck's the matter? You look like you've seen the Devil himself."

"I think I have," O'Grady replied. "In fact, I'm sure I have."

Fallon had led him to the nearest café, bought him coffee, sat him down. "So, fella, tell me everything."

So he did.

Fallon had sipped his coffee, listened in silence. Then he'd spoken. "One day, Finn. One day we will tell this story straight. We will make sure the world knows what these men have done. It may take time, but one day we will see justice done."

CHAPTER 17

O'GRADY LOOKED AROUND THE wreckage of his dream home.

I caused that man's death. But it was Hawthorne who pulled the trigger.

O'Grady heard footsteps behind him. He spun round, his hand clapped on his pistol.

Vera Joyce was walking towards him, taking careful steps along the path.

"I thought I might find you here," she said.

"Miss Joyce—"

She smiled. "You can call me Vera if you like. We've known each other long enough."

He looked at his shoes. "Just—just the way I was brought up, I guess…"

She surveyed the shell of the house in the slanting afternoon light. "Poor Mr. Elliott," she said at last. "It was here, wasn't it? That—"

"That he died, yes."

"Hawthorne and his thugs," she said. "And not one of us able to tell the truth."

He stared at the ground.

"I knew the Devlin boys," she said. "From my teaching. The odd thing is, they were sweet kids. Rough-hewn but gentle as puppies. They'd knock the daylights out of each other, but they'd never hurt another soul. Not then, anyway."

"What changed them?" O'Grady asked.

"It must be the money. I can't see why else they chose the path they did. They came from a lovely home." She smiled. "Their mother sewed quilts—she was chairwoman of the Galway Needlecraft Guild. And their father ran the local allotments. A devoted couple. But their sons became hired criminals. They even changed their names, you know. They were christened Sebastian and Ignatius, after the saints. Good holy names. Swapped for those silly tags, as if they're playing at being gangsters."

He nodded.

"So much suffering," she went on. She looked at the bare brick, the gap in the wall where the fireplace would have been. "And yet, some of us overcome our suffering." She stood, slight in her dark gray dress. "It's strange, isn't it," she said. "How some people have known great darkness in their lives and yet manage to live in the light. And others allow the darkness to engulf them. The O'Connor boys," she said. "Stuart and Sean. Now there's an example. Two such different paths they took. I taught them both. Their father…" She shook her head. "They should have been taken away from that house. They'd have been better off—well, anywhere else. Anywhere at all. Their father was a nasty, selfish man. He was obsessed with his collection.

First World War memorabilia. He didn't like anything to get in the way of it. He didn't like his wife. He didn't like his boys. Sean was a gentle soul. Stuart was that bit tougher. But that's how Stuart managed to survive, I reckon. He went on to marry, have a child, and what a good father he was to little Bobby, a good father…" She stopped, breathed. Her eyes went to the distant trees, as if she was collecting her thoughts. "But Sean"— she turned back to O'Grady—"he behaves like someone who doesn't trust the world to be safe. That's why he hangs about with the tough guys. That's why he takes refuge in money. Why, he'd sell his best friend if he thought it would earn him a few euros. 'No one can hurt you if you're rich,' he used to say."

She ran her finger along the dusty brickwork. "Ah, well. Here's me chattering away. What I came here to say…" She looked up at him. "I came here to say, I don't think what's happening—these awful events—I don't think it's anything to do with the Green Man. It's not that I don't believe in the old tales—I believe in them more than anyone can know. But it's a sideshow, in my view. There's some real harm going on, someone evil meaning business." She touched his arm. "That's what I wanted to say. Evil begets evil." She walked to the door, then turned back. "Do you know, Stuart O'Connor told me that during the beatings, his mother would stand in the kitchen singing, loudly, to drown out the boys' screams? 'Danny Boy,' she'd sing." She gave a small shudder. "And yet Stuart managed to transcend it, grow beyond it. You can never tell."

Vera paused. "You shouldn't blame yourself. For…" She gestured to the space around them. "For what happened here. The truth will out. I have faith that it will." She smiled. "I must go. I took little Bobby back to his mother, but I know she wants to get on." Vera walked away, back towards the town.

O'Grady leaned against the wall and watched her pick her way along the track until she was out of sight.

Evil begets evil.

He looked down, tried not to see the bloodstained image of his friend seared across the shadows.

It is time, he thought. *I have waited too long.*

He left the old site and walked back up the hill. He found Bridie in the garden, picking blackberries. He joined her, adding handfuls of dark fruit to her basket.

After lunch, washing up with her in the kitchen, O'Grady turned to Bridie. "Tell me," he said. "If there were no Salters, who would inherit this farm?"

She stood in the thin sunlight of the kitchen. "There's only Jason and myself left, but if we were to go it would be my next of kin—Bobby. But until Bobby is of age…" Her voice faltered as the truth dawned. "His next of kin would hold the lease for him. It would be his uncle."

"Sean O'Connor," O'Grady said. "Who puts money before everything else. Who needs the land for the mill race, so he has a water supply for his golf course. With his friend Kiley MacAteer, the man who murdered your sister."

She was trembling as she faced him. "Finn. You must warn Jason."

"I've tried. He wouldn't listen."

She grasped his arm. "So try again."

O'Grady looked down at her. "You're right," he said. "The past. All those wrongs. It's over. I was angry in the past. I'm even angrier now." He stepped away, went out of the room, out of the house.

She heard the slam of the Audi door, the engine revving away into the distance.

CHAPTER 18

O'GRADY PUSHED THROUGH THE heavy brass doors of the Garda HQ.

May Riley was on reception. Same smart white blouse, same bright red lipstick.

"I guess you're going to walk straight past me again," she said.

"I'm just that kind of guy," he replied, and she laughed.

This time O'Grady didn't knock. Hawthorne was standing, staring out of the window. He turned. "How the fuck did you get in here?"

"The same way as last time," O'Grady said.

"Well, you can go out the same fucking way then."

"Hawthorne, the game's over. I've had enough."

Hawthorne gave a mirthless laugh. "You know what, O'Grady? No one gives a shit what you think."

"You know who killed Maura Salter, and it wasn't that poor sap who did time for it and died in jail. You know that Gregson Elliott had information concerning you and your friend Mac-Ateer, which is why you had to put a stop to him."

Hawthorne lowered himself into the chair behind his desk. He surveyed O'Grady with his characteristic sneer. "This again? Do you remember what happened last time you went down this road? It was the end of you, O'Grady. Disgraced. I told you if you tried any such thing again I'd have you arrested. I meant it."

His hand went to a bell by his desk, some kind of push-button.

"I don't think so." O'Grady stood in front of him. "I'm ready to start talking about what happened that night Maura died."

Hawthorne leaned back in his chair, his plump fingers inter-linked across his waistcoat. "And who will listen to you? No one believed you then, and no one will believe you now. Who are you, O'Grady? You're no one. A disgraced police officer."

O'Grady's hands tightened into fists at his side.

"As for that American lad," Hawthorne went on. "I showed great restraint not having you thrown into a cell for the rest of your life."

"Because you knew the case wouldn't stand up, Hawthorne." O'Grady's voice was ice cold. "I had no motive. Whereas you— you had every reason to get that fella out of the way, because he was the only one who knew what happened the night Maura Sal-ter died. Gregson was about to tell me. Sean O'Connor had let slip that you were out and about that night with Kiley MacAteer."

Hawthorne gave a rattling laugh. "These are tall tales, O'Grady. Where's the evidence? You, you were the one found at the scene of the crime, gun in your fingers, a man dead at your feet, in your property." His arm shot out towards the bell. Be-fore he could reach it, O'Grady had grasped his wrist with both hands and twisted it, hard. Hawthorne's face grew red with rage and pain.

"I haven't finished, Brian," he said. "These killings of the Salter men." He increased the pressure on Hawthorne's wrist. Hawthorne's face tightened, his lips working. "I have been biding my time," O'Grady said. "It might have looked to you like I was doing nothing at all. But I know exactly what's happening here."

Hawthorne was breathing heavily. With his other hand he tried to reach for the bell. "I think it's time you left, O'Grady," he said, thick-voiced, as O'Grady's mobile rang, loud in the stuffy room.

Bridie's ringtone. He dropped his hold of Hawthorne and snatched up his phone.

"Fire!" she was shouting. "The ghost estate. It's Jason! Fire! Get there. Please!"

CHAPTER 19

O'GRADY DROVE FAST OUT of town, back to the estate. He could see the smoke before he smelt it, a thick darkness against the stormy sunset sky.

There was an oily, burning stench in the air as he slammed the car door.

The shell of the golf club house was leaping with flames. There were fire engines, police cars, jets of water crisscrossing the orange smoke.

Bridie was standing, watching the blaze. O'Grady ran to her side and she grasped his arm. "I smelt the smoke," she said. "I knew. I ran here. There was a huge explosion." Her voice was flat. "Jason's in there...." She nodded her head towards the last building, its empty windows licked with flames. "I'm next."

His arms were on her shoulders. "No," he said.

"Water," she said. "That'll be me."

He put his arms around her, but she was rigid, unyielding.

"I won't let you die," he said.

The buildings flickered with fire as the sky grew dark. Headlights cut through the smoke. And now two firefighters made their way into the burned-out golf club, fighting through the rubble.

After a long moment, they reappeared, carrying between them a body. O'Grady saw the charred skin, the scalp raw between the remaining patches of blond hair.

Bridie stood motionless, gazing blankly at the scene before them. They laid the body on a stretcher. The firemen stood, one at each side, as if paying their respects. Then they picked up the stretcher and carried Jason to a waiting ambulance.

O'Grady felt Bridie stumble at his side. He caught her, his arms strong around her. He led her away to his car.

CHAPTER 20

HE PARKED OUTSIDE THE farmhouse. Bridie got out of the car and walked ahead of him.

The house was warm and light. Bobby was sitting by the hearth, pushing a toy fire engine up and down, making vroom-vroom noises. In the kitchen, Vera was washing up their supper dishes.

Bridie went to her son, lifted him into her arms and held him close.

"You smell smoky," he said to her. He sniffed at her. "I like that smell."

She buried her face in his soft hair. "I'll put him to bed," she said and carried him upstairs.

Vera appeared from the kitchen carrying a bottle of claret and two glasses.

"You'll be needing a drink," she said. She poured a glass for O'Grady and one for herself. "I'd say *sláinte*," she said, raising her glass, "only it's not that sort of night."

"*Sláinte agad-sa,*" he replied.

She sat down opposite him. "Thank you for putting up with

my chatter earlier," she said. "Sometimes I find myself weighed down with thinking." She picked up her glass, watched the light filter through the crystal red. "I'm glad you're here," she said. "Bridie has very few friends."

He waited.

"She doesn't help herself," she said. She surveyed him, as if making a decision, then spoke again. "I may be speaking out of turn. But my thinking is, it's guilt. After Maura's awful death, the violence of it all. Bridie was only a year or so older than her, but she always felt responsible for her. And the boys didn't help, retreating into that masculine posturing, just like their grandfather. It left Bridie and her father to carry all the grief, the shame, even. You know what it's like, a sexual assault in a town like this, there's always a darkness about it, as if the poor girl was somehow to blame."

From upstairs they could hear Bobby's laughter, and then singing, Bridie's sweet voice. *"Seoithín, seo hó, mo stór é, mo leanbh…"*

Vera spoke again. "Mr. O'Grady, I am entirely in agreement with you regarding these recent deaths. Someone is using the story of the Green Man and its history with this family as a cover. And yet it's a terrible misreading of the story. It's what I said before. The Green Man is all about redemption, the being who dies so that new life can begin. He's like the spring, the seeds growing in the earth. Why do you think St. Patrick's Day falls at the March equinox? It's the same idea, the celebration of a holy man who redeems us." She shook her head. "Whoever's doing this knows nothing." She fell silent.

He sipped his wine. "Miss Joyce," he said. "What was James Salter like?"

Her eyes darkened at his name. "A terrible man. A horrible man. He left an awful legacy in this family."

"You knew him well?"

She gave a nod. "When his wife was ill, I came to nurse her. I was only a teenager—Richard and I were about the same age. Then Mary died and then James. I was glad when he died. Everyone was."

"How did you get involved in Richard's research?"

She smiled. "I went away to college, did my stint at teaching. When I came back, there was Richard, married now, doing his wonderful work. And so I helped him. Those were happy times," she said. "Happy times." Her smile faded. "Up until the dreadful tragedy of Maura." She flashed him a glance. "Not a tragedy, of course. Worse than that. A terrible, terrible evil…" Her voice sharpened. "To think there is a man still alive who knows that poor girl's last moments, her pain and suffering, who caused it, delighted in it, found his pleasure in it…" Her voice cracked. Her hand fluttered to her face. She covered her eyes. "I'm sorry," she murmured.

"Miss Joyce," he said. "It's quite all right. I feel exactly the same as you do."

She composed herself, reached for her glass of wine. "It added to the Salter sense of guilt," she said. "Richard's work was authentic, about Irish stories, Irish truths. But he kept this belief that somehow his family had stolen something from the very earth itself." She looked up. "We're given to superstition, we Irish, that's the problem. Even now. Do you know, I caught Sean O'Connor and his business friends the other day, up on the hill there; one of them asked me about ghosts on the estate and if I thought holy water would protect against them, and if Father Anthony from St. Joseph's would come and sprinkle some on their building site!" She laughed, then shook her head. "They're just fools, of course. Dangerous fools, but fools none the less. Poor, dear Bridie, she's allowed all these stories to warp her mind…I don't know how to help her." She sighed. "I'm hoping you do," she said, her bright eyes fixed on his.

"I hope so too," he said.

There were footsteps on the stairs. Bridie appeared, hollow-eyed with exhaustion. She collapsed into a chair. Vera poured her a glass of wine.

They sat in silence. After a while, Vera got to her feet. "I'll leave you in peace," she said. "My cats need to remember who I am. There's half a shepherd's pie in the oven. It'll still be warm." She touched Bridie's shoulder. "I'll see you tomorrow." She glanced at O'Grady, gathered up her coat, went out of the door.

"I'm not hungry," Bridie said.

"Nor me."

A coal shifted in the grate. Outside there was the hoot of an owl.

O'Grady looked at Bridie. "I never stopped loving you," he said.

She raised her eyes to him. Her face glowed in the warmth

of the fire. "Finn," she said. She hesitated, reached across, took hold of his hand. "I'm a wife," she said. "I made vows."

"A widow," he said.

"A vow of faithfulness…" she said.

"Till death us do part," he said.

She shook her head. "I am not free," she said. She got to her feet. "I can't expect you to understand. But I am not mine to give."

She turned away. He heard her light step on the stairs.

He sipped his wine and thought about Gregson Elliott. *The only thing he would have wanted to tell me was the truth of Maura's death.*

Sean O'Connor knew we were meeting that night. He was the only person who could have known that Gregson was heading for my hut. And now here he is, strutting around the ghost estate with MacAteer.

O'Grady sat by the window, watching the moon through the window. He thought about the distant weir, that constant rush of water. He thought about the waterwheel, once at the heart of the Salter business, now reduced to a useless mechanism of cogs and wheels. He thought about young Bobby, all these generations later, taking such delight in their orderly circling. He had a sense of a thought taking shape, of things falling into place.

CHAPTER 21

EARLY ON SUNDAY MORNING, O'Grady went to the ghost estate.

The mist hung in the air, over the chill earth, the desolate houses. Smoke still drifted from the husk of the golf club.

He could hear church bells ringing in the distance, calling the faithful to prayer. He paced the bleak land between the houses, the heavy scent of burned oil hanging in the air.

A figure was coming into focus, through the mist. Sean O'Connor, he realized. At first Sean didn't see him. He walked towards the derelict golf club and came to a standstill, staring at the blackened roof.

O'Grady approached him.

Sean heard his footsteps on the track. He turned, fists clenched, then breathed. "Oh," he said. "It's only you."

"And who were you expecting, Sean?"

"No one." Sean was sullen-faced.

"Just as well it's only me, then."

Sean eyed him.

"What have they promised you, O'Connor—your friends, MacAteer and Hawthorne? What have they said you'll gain by all this?"

"Don't know what you mean."

"You're tainting yourself with evil, Sean. Contaminating your very soul. You should get away from those men."

Sean flicked him an uncertain glance. "I know who I trust with my business," he said.

"Business? You call this business?" O'Grady waved an arm across the site. "MacAteer needs you for one thing only," he said.

"Oh? And what's that?" Sean blustered.

O'Grady pointed down the hill, towards the river, the old mill building. "Water," he said. "He knows damn well this land is worthless to him without that water supply."

Sean blinked.

"They're not interested in helping you make money, Sean," O'Grady went on. "They're using you, for the Salter inheritance."

"You're talking fucking crap, O'Grady."

"I'm telling you the truth. And you know it. And even if you wanted to escape, I'll wager they're telling you there's no way out. Not after Gregson's death and your part in it."

Sean put up a hand against the wall, as if to steady himself. "You can go to the Devil, O'Grady. Murphy was a friend of mine."

"The night that Maura Salter died, you were the only person other than Gregson who knew her whereabouts. There you were, hammering away on your roof with Gregson, and him chatting happily about how he was going to meet her at the bus stop as usual. Who else was there to hear? Only you, O'Connor, only you."

"What's all this to me?" Sean was shouting now.

"And then Gregson was hounded out of town, in fear of his life. But before he left, he agreed to meet me. He was going to tell me everything he knew, about the killing of Maura Salter, and the part you played."

"I did nothing—"

"You tipped off your friends. How much did Hawthorne pay you? A hundred? Fifty? Ten?"

Sean squared his shoulders, readying himself to fight. "You're a fucking loser, O'Grady. I started with nothing and I made something of my life."

"You mean this? These worthless shells?"

Sean's eyes narrowed. "If anyone's responsible for the death of Gregson Elliott, it's you. You were the one who lured him to your house—"

"Shut it right there, O'Connor. You and I both know who pulled that trigger to silence him. You told Hawthorne where to find him. You sold your friend for thirty pieces of silver. You're on the road to hell, O'Connor, when you could have chosen a better path, like your brother did—"

"Don't bring my brother into this."

"Despite your father's violence, despite the beatings—"

"What are you saying?" Sean raised his fist, ready to throw a punch.

"'Danny Boy,' was it? That your mother used to sing?"

"How fucking dare you—"

O'Grady began to sing. "Oh, Danny boy, the pipes, the pipes are calling—"

Sean aimed a punch at his chest. O'Grady deflected it and delivered a sharp upper cut. Sean stumbled backwards. He stood, breathing hard.

"You can fight me all you like, O'Connor, but it's not going to stop me. Not now. I've had it with you and your friends. And talk of the Devil—here they are."

Kiley MacAteer was walking towards them, flanked by two figures. Stig and Dooley Devlin came into focus through the mist.

"Spot of trouble, O'Connor?" MacAteer stopped, eyeing O'Grady.

O'Grady faced him. "We were just chewing over the past, weren't we? Reminiscing like two old fellas."

Sean's eyes flashed rage.

"I'm surprised you dare to show yourself here, MacAteer," O'Grady said.

"I own this land."

"Yeah? At what cost?"

MacAteer gave his hoarse laugh. "Get the hell out of here, O'Grady, while you still have a choice."

"Are you going to make me?" O'Grady met his eyes. "Or will you keep hiding behind your hired prizefighters here?"

The Devlin brothers shifted on their heavy feet.

MacAteer gave another empty laugh. "You're powerless,

O'Grady. You know you are. This land is mine. Anything I want, I get."

"You didn't get Maura Salter. And you decided no one else would have her either."

A theatrical sigh from MacAteer. "These old, tired lies, O'Grady."

"And you two." O'Grady turned to the brothers. "How much did Hawthorne pay you to take care of Gregson Elliott?"

The Devlin twins exchanged childish grins.

"Oh, Stig, Dooley," O'Grady said. "What would your poor mother make of you now? Sitting with her quilting, so proud of her sons when you were small. So little to be proud of now. Which of you was Sebastian, then? And which Ignatius?"

Their smiles vanished. They stared at O'Grady.

MacAteer looked at them. "No," he said. "Really?" He laughed his mocking laugh. "Sebastian and Ignatius," he repeated.

"After the saints," O'Grady explained.

"The saints," MacAteer echoed. He jerked his head back towards the road. "You can go and sit in the van, you two. St. Stig and St. Dooley," he laughed, as they turned to go.

The two men lumbered away, hunched like sulking children.

MacAteer looked at O'Grady. "How did you find that out, then?"

O'Grady smiled. "Oh, you know. We Gardaí. There's lots we know. Isn't there, Sean?"

Sean was leaning against the wall, gazing after the Devlin twins. He shrugged.

"Which is why I know you're behind the Salter deaths," O'Grady said.

MacAteer's smile died. "These lies again, O'Grady. They mean nothing to me. Tall stories, all of 'em."

"And what about the other stories, MacAteer? What about the Green Man?"

An uneasy glance flicked between Sean and MacAteer.

"You've seen him too, then," O'Grady hazarded. "After all, something must have made you ask about sprinkling holy water on the building site."

O'Connor stared at the ground. MacAteer was silent.

"Last night, was it?" O'Grady went on. "Yesterday afternoon, perhaps. Through the smoke of the fire you set? As the soul left the body of Jason Salter—"

"That's enough." It was O'Connor, shouting. "I said, that's enough."

"Or perhaps you just heard him," O'Grady went on. "The strange singing that everyone says you hear when he passes."

MacAteer stepped forwards. "Get out," he said. "Get away from here."

O'Grady's fists were clenched at his sides, but then he heard someone calling his name, "Mr. O'Grady." A woman's voice. He turned to see Vera running towards them. "It's Bridie," she was saying. "She's gone missing. I think she's at the mill race. I've left Bobby with my neighbor, Mrs. Friel. I came as soon as I could."

CHAPTER 22

VERA RAN AHEAD, DOWN the hill, towards the old waterwheel. The stream was high, the waves crashing downwards.

Water, O'Grady thought. *The fourth element. The fourth cause of death.*

He could hear a soft, lyrical singing. It took him a moment to realize it was coming from a female form, standing by the water's edge.

"Bridie," he said, breathing with relief.

"Bridie!" Vera called to her.

She seemed not to hear them. *"Seoithín, seo hó, mo stór é, mo leanbh…"* she was singing. "Hush-a-bye, baby, my darling, my child…."

Vera turned to O'Grady. "I'm so worried about her. After her sister…after the…after the thing happened, after she died, Bridie would stand here for hours." She went up to Bridie and put an arm gently around her. Bridie blinked, turned to her and seemed to see them both for the first time.

"Come on," Vera said. "Let's go home."

*   *   *

They tucked Bridie into bed, and she fell into a deep sleep. Vera retrieved Bobby from her neighbor. The day drew on. Bobby played on the hearthrug with a wooden puzzle. Vera chopped onions and sliced a lamb shoulder for a casserole.

"That man," O'Grady said, peeling carrots. "That evil man. Striding around the neighborhood."

"He got away with it. He got away with the murder of beautiful Maura and he's getting away with it still." Vera's voice was raised. "That's what I can't bear."

"I tried," O'Grady said. "I tried to bring him to justice—"

They stopped, hearing Bridie's step on the stairs. She seemed calmer now, as she went to Bobby, helped him with his puzzle. O'Grady lit the fire.

The casserole was eaten with baked potatoes. Bobby went to bed after Teddy Peter had insisted it was time, with O'Grady putting on the voice again—a fire-and-brimstone preacher he seemed to have become, but Bobby still laughed.

Vera agreed she would stay. She went to the back door and drew the bolts across.

"I'm taking no chances," she said. "And you should have curtains on these," she said, pointing to the large bay windows. "Just because your dear pa said this room was for living in, not hiding in. Curtains would make it homely."

Bridie looked up. "One day," she said.

"Get me some nice red velvet and I'll sew them for you," Vera said. "Or maybe a fifties print, Festival of Britain…"

Bridie smiled, and for a moment the room settled, calmed.

But as Vera went to the front door and turned the key in the lock, the air around them tightened again.

"Sleep well, my dear." Vera patted Bridie's arm and tiptoed away up to the spare bedroom.

Bridie looked at O'Grady. Her eyes were hollow with fear. She went to him and touched his shoulder. "I can't sleep alone," she said. "Will you come with me?"

Wordlessly, she led him to her room.

CHAPTER 23

O'GRADY LAY NEXT TO Bridie in the wide double bed with its fine linen sheets. The moon washed the room with silver light.

Bridie, still dressed, had lain down and almost immediately fallen into a deep, exhausted sleep. He watched her, not daring to touch her; her fine features, her hair spread across the lace-edged pillows. He felt a wave of tenderness towards her.

The house was still. The night was silent.

Suddenly there was a click of the gate. A faint step on the path.

O'Grady was out of bed and on his feet.

The window lock downstairs rattled.

O'Grady went to his jacket and picked up his gun. Noise-lessly, he slipped out of the room and made his way down the stairs.

The living room was in darkness except for the moonlight streaming through the uncurtained windows.

A crunch of a step outside.

A shadow crossed the window.

A face. A wide, green-hued face, eyes staring out from a mask of leaves, a mane of tangled twigs, a mocking smile.

O'Grady stared, unable to believe what he was seeing. The

face stared back. And then he heard it, the growling hum of the song coming through the windowpane.

O'Grady watched, transfixed. His fingers touched the handle of his Glock.

A soft step in the room behind him, a gasp, a scream. He whirled. Bridie was standing, her hands on her face, her eyes wide with terror.

A loud thump as the Green Man's fist hit the window.

O'Grady ran to the door, wrenched the lock open and ran outside.

The masked figure had fled and was nowhere to be seen.

O'Grady heard a footstep behind him. He whipped round, saw a male figure, raised his gun and fired.

The man fell. But from the trees came laughter, and then, again, the low notes of the Green Man's song.

O'Grady stood in the shadows of the garden. The man he had shot was still breathing, his chest rattling. O'Grady took a step towards him, but then, behind him, he heard the cock of another pistol.

Again O'Grady turned, saw a second figure lumbering towards him, and fired. The figure shouted, a raucous male voice, and fell forwards.

It was as if time had slowed. Then the singing again. And now the Green Man emerged once more, a looming shadow. He unlatched the garden gate as if coming home, his uneven grin a slash across his face. In front of him, pointed directly at O'Grady, he held a hunting rifle.

His singing stopped. He took aim and fired.

But O'Grady had fired first.

The Green Man fell, his bullet hitting the wall behind O'Grady in a hail of plaster.

There was silence. The rattling breathing had stopped. A low moan came from the second, injured man. On the path the Green Man lay twitching, gurgling. Then he too quietened and grew still.

O'Grady let his arm drop to his side. He breathed, turned slowly round.

Bridie was standing in the doorway, rigid with terror. O'Grady walked towards her and took her in his arms. "Bridie…my love," he murmured. "Everything is going to be all right. I know who these men are."

CHAPTER 24

O'GRADY PULLED OUT A torch and shone it on the first man, who was now lifeless, his eyes staring. "Sean O'Connor," O'Grady said. He crouched down next to him. "A coward's life. Your tip-offs, your gossip. Your thirty pieces of silver. All ending with a young man burned to death."

He got to his feet. "And as for you…" He walked over to the second man, who was lying, moaning, cursing, his heavy body sprawled across the grass. "Brian Hawthorne," O'Grady said. "I've no doubt you would have aimed to kill me. But don't worry, boy—I'll call you an ambulance. Perhaps."

In reply, Hawthorne, twisted with pain, spat out a few grunts of hatred.

"And this…" O'Grady stepped over to where the Green Man lay, lifeless. "What plot was this that these three hatched? To terrify the Salters. To inherit the Salter land. And to get me out of the way once and for all. Just to make sure their scheme couldn't fail. And here we are.…" He bent down, his hand on the mask. It was made of green plastic, with holes for eyes and mouth, on which had been glued a collection of leaves and twigs. He lifted it away. "Kiley MacAteer," O'Grady said. "His greed was beyond limits. His cruelty made victims of everyone he touched. Well, it's over now."

Bridie was at his side, staring down at the half-open eyes, the blue lips, the trickle of blood from the corner of his mouth.

O'Grady straightened up, holding the mask. He turned towards Bridie. "Justice for your sister. At last."

Bobby had woken, and now stumbled through the door, searching for his mother. Behind him Vera ran to catch him, crouched down next to him to prevent him getting any nearer, enfolding him in her arms.

"Mammy," he called, and Bridie went to him, and held him. "Everything's all right," she said. She turned to Vera. "I'm calling an ambulance. One of them is still alive."

She went into the house. Bobby looked up at O'Grady, at the mask he was holding in his hand. He broke away from Vera, ran to O'Grady and reached up to it. O'Grady handed him the mask. Bobby studied it, holding it in his small, steady fingers. Then he passed it back to O'Grady. He shook his head. "This wasn't the one in my dream," he said. "The one I saw was a special one, a magic one, like a real tree. This is just a silly one."

CHAPTER 25

THE AMBULANCE CAME. HAWTHORNE was stretchered away, his consciousness fading from blood loss, but still uttering threats of vengeance.

The ambulance drove away into the night. Then came the police, DS Driscoll and DC Laverty again. "Getting to be a habit hanging around the Salter residence," O'Grady said to them. DC Laverty gave a thin smile. DS Driscoll took out a notebook. "There are quite a lot of questions I need to ask you, Mr. O'Grady," he said.

O'Grady led them into the house. They sat in the dim light of the front room.

"Yes," O'Grady said. "I fired. Three times."

"You killed two men," DS Driscoll said.

"Yes," he replied.

DC Laverty was trying not to stare.

"You injured Chief Super Hawthorne," Driscoll went on. "Did you mean to kill him?"

O'Grady shook his head. "I didn't want him dead."

"But the others—you shot to kill?"

O'Grady looked at DS Driscoll. "They'd come armed. They

wanted me dead. It was self-defense." He leaned back in his seat. "And I shall argue that in court. Am I under arrest?"

The two young officers glanced at each other.

"You can arrest me now," O'Grady said, "or you can come back whenever you like. I'm not going anywhere."

Bridie had appeared from upstairs. He saw her flicker of a smile.

The two officers got to their feet. "We are instructing you to report to Garda HQ first thing in the morning. Is that clear?" DS Driscoll looked firmly at O'Grady.

"Yes, officers. That is perfectly clear."

He showed them to the door. They left with a breath of relief.

Vera came downstairs. "He's asleep," she said to Bridie. "He seems perfectly calm now."

Bridie made a pot of tea. They sat at the kitchen table in the warmth of the range.

Once Vera had gone to bed, Bridie and O'Grady sat in silence. Outside it was still night. She stirred her spoon around in her mug, then turned to him. "Justice for my sister," she said. "At last." She reached across and took hold of his hand. She raised it to her lips, kissing each finger. She looked across at him, her eyes dark with yearning. "Justice," she said again. "And now I'm free."

CHAPTER 26

O'GRADY LAY AWAKE NEXT to Bridie. He felt himself very much in love with her. Like at the beginning, he thought. As if the years between had simply faded away.

She was fast asleep, the sheets draped across her naked form. He watched her soft breathing, the curves of her body, her silky skin.

Outside, the dawn was just beginning to break, a blur of pale blue at the edges of the sky.

He looked up and stared at the ceiling. He was aware of feeling anxious, a sense of dread.

But why? he thought. *Why this feeling that the story isn't over?*

He got up, restless, went out onto the landing in the early dawn light.

The door to Bobby's room was wide open.

O'Grady ran into the room. The bed was empty, the covers pulled back. The window was flung wide, the curtains twitching in the breeze.

He went to the window. A ladder led down from it into the garden.

He ran to Bridie, shook her. "He's gone, Bobby—"

She was bolt upright in terror. "Water," she said. "Oh, my God. Water."

"But they're dead," O'Grady said. "O'Connor, MacAteer. And Hawthorne's in hospital—"

"Water," she said again. "Don't you see? This is the real Green Man. I was right."

"I don't believe in ghosts," O'Grady said. "Come on." He dragged her downstairs, draped a coat around her, pushed her in front of him outside to the car.

"Where are we going?"

"We're going to the only place that makes any sense," he said. "While there's still time."

CHAPTER 27

THE WEIR WAS A sheer drop, falling away from the old red-brick mill, its foaming water rushing downwards against the stones.

They could see him, Bobby, a tiny figure in the gray dawn light, standing apparently alone, inches from the edge.

Then they saw, behind him, a ghostly figure. A green robe, a mask of leaves and branches, an interweaving of greenery. Fiery eyes seemed to peer out from the foliage. The figure was singing, a low, guttural song.

Its arm was extended, as if about to push Bobby into the weir.

"Bobby!" Bridie shouted.

The boy turned and saw her. He appeared unafraid. Behind him the Green Man's hand darted outwards. At the same moment, O'Grady fired. The monster crumpled to the ground.

Bobby screamed and fled into his mother's arms.

O'Grady ran to the wounded figure, which even now was stumbling to its feet. O'Grady could see that this Green Man, unlike the clumsy giant of Kiley MacAteer, was really very small.

"You are no ghost," he said, his hand reaching out to the mask.

Before he could touch it, the figure put its hand up and took off the mask. Standing there, shaking with shock, bleeding heavily, was Vera Joyce.

Bobby looked at her, tears streaming down his face. "Nana Vee said we'd go and see the cogwheels. She said it was a treat...." He looked up at O'Grady. "Why did you hurt her?"

CHAPTER 28

BRIDIE HELD HER SON tight in her arms as he sobbed. O'Grady went to Vera and helped her to sit down, putting his jacket around her shoulders.

Bridie began to speak, her voice weak with shock. "Why?"

Vera was pale but her words were clear. "The end of the Salters," she said. "My singing will see them out of this world and into the darkness."

"But…" O'Grady shook his head. "You've loved the Salters…."

"Richard," she said. "But even Richard was too weak to overcome the evil of his father. I was only fifteen when I started working for James Salter," she said. "I knew nothing about life. A country girl. I knew it was wrong, but who could I tell? The priest would tell me I was sinful. I thought I was sinful. James would tell me it was my fault for being a temptress, even though it was him forcing me, hurting me, time after time…." Her voice weakened. O'Grady adjusted his coat around her shoulders.

"Then he got ill and old, and it stopped. And then he died. By then I knew…I knew the harm he'd done. I knew I couldn't have children. And my mind…it was as if he'd put thoughts there, devil's thoughts, like threads of badness woven through my thinking…." She stopped, breathed. "But Richard was kind, and gave me work, work that followed my own passions, about singing and dance and the old stories. I was happy, in a way. The devil threads, they lessened, diminished. I was happy to see Richard married to Ellen, I was happy when his children came along, although it was true that James was present still in the behavior of the boys. But Bridie here…" She smiled at Bridie, a brief glow of warmth in her eyes.

"But…" Her face shadowed. "The demons were always there. I was so harmed, so angry…those times with—with him, when I was so young, so confused, sometimes those memories would appear in my mind as if they were happening now, right now, that hurt, that shame, that pleading for him to stop, please stop, and his voice, mocking, abusing, saying words, nasty devil words, what he was about to do…" She stopped, a breathing sob, then continued.

"I might have done nothing. Nothing at all. I might have taken all that evil to my grave. Even when that terrible harm came to Maura, that brought it all back, even then I did nothing. But then I overheard Sean one day, out near the estate, talking to that evil MacAteer man, and they were worrying about ghosts. Funny how people can be. They were worrying about the land beneath those new houses, and the old stories about it being cursed. They asked me about holy water. And so I told them about the Green Man, the spirit of the earth, who will always rise again. I saw it in their eyes, their greed. What they would be willing to do. And so I planted a seed, a germ of an idea, about hauntings and revenge, and how the Green Man will claim his land for himself. And sure enough, some days later, Sean came to me and asked me lots of questions—what did the Green Man look like—and I told him. I told him about the singing, I did some for him, the ancient chant, and he recorded it on his phone. I had this mask, a Green Man mask from my research with Richard." She touched it as it lay at her side. "He'd brought it from Canterbury or somewhere. I got it out, and Sean stared at it, studied it. I think it frightened him...." She gave a small smile.

"After Sean had gone, I sat there, thinking and thinking, and it was like my mind was allowing all that pain to fill the space, and all I could think was, it is justice at last, the end of the Salter line. I knew what they were planning—Sean had let slip about ghosts and lineage. I knew what he meant, though I don't think he realized what he'd betrayed.... That night I took the mask, and I tried it out—that's when Bobby saw it. And then I sat back and waited. All I had to do was wait." She managed another smile, although she was chalk white and trembling now. "They made their plastic Green Man mask. They copied my song. They sang it very badly. Sometimes I would hide nearby and sing it for real. It frightened them." She gave a weak laugh.

"We must get you an ambulance," Bridie said.

Vera glanced at Bridie, at Bobby curled in her arms. She

spoke again. "He would take me here, your grandfather. To the old mill. I didn't know how to argue with him. I've never told anyone about this before, ever. He would say I was bad, he'd tell me it was my fault, that I deserved it.... After a while I didn't know how else to think about it. And now, when I bring little Bobby here, and I watch him playing with the machine, so happy…" She reached up, her hand touching her hair. "My thoughts all go wrong. Your grandfather did such bad things to me here...." She took a breath, went on. "Your sweet, innocent boy there, your dear son…I wanted him dead. That's how evil I am."

"Vera—you need help," Bridie said.

Vera shook her head. "There's one part of the story you don't know," she said. "Six months ago, I was told I had cancer. It started in my brain. It's everywhere now. I don't have long to live." She lurched unevenly to her feet. "I don't want to die that way."

She stood, looking down at Bridie and Bobby. She limped over to him and stroked his head. "I used to look at this sweet boy here and think, if there was a God, He would not have allowed this. I was deprived of motherhood. That wicked man stole my faith, my hope, and he left devils lurking within me. He forced me to carry his guilt and yet had none at all himself. It gave me anger, like an illness—I couldn't contain it, all that hatred, that shame. But now…" She took a step away. "It's funny," she said. "It's all gone. I look within my heart and I feel only peace."

She surveyed them all. "For all these years, I've been unable to see clearly. I've looked at this child, and all I've been able to see is the evil that was done to me by that man. But now…Now all shall be well." She smiled. "I am guilty of one crime only, and that is a crime against the Green Man himself." She picked up the mask, leaned it against the wall behind her. "I warped his story when I told it to the O'Connor boy. I made it a story of vengeance and killing, when the truth of the Green Man is about renewal and hope, and the warmth of the earth allowing life to live once more. But I'm sure he will forgive me that. In fact, I know he has…"

She took a sudden rush of steps towards the mill race. O'Grady lunged towards her, grabbing at her green skirts as they floated out behind her like a sail. But she slipped through his grasp and disappeared, down into the depths.

CHAPTER 29

BRIDIE TURNED TO O'GRADY. "What do we do now?" she said. "Do we walk away?"

He watched the tumbling stream. "There's a woman down there...."

"Finn—we can't help her. Not now."

He pulled out his phone.

"The police?" she said. "What if they take you away from me?"

He punched in a number. "Don't worry," he said. "They won't."

She heard him speak into his phone. He clicked it off. "Come on," he said. "We'll wait. We can watch the cogwheels."

Bobby stared blankly towards the water. Bridie bent, cradled him in her arms. Then she went over to the mask and picked it up.

"What are you going to do with that?"

She looked at it. "He's coming with us. It's what Vera said. The Green Man is a story of redemption and hope. And God knows we need it now."

The sun was high in the sky when they saw the cars arriving at the watermill. Two cars, a yellow-striped Mondeo patrol car, and an unmarked black Volvo. The Volvo slid silently to a halt. The doors opened. A figure got out, a broad, tall man in a dark suit and thick boots.

He took a step towards O'Grady. He held out his arm. "Didn't I always say, if you need me, call."

O'Grady went to greet him, grasped his hand. "Fallon," he said. "Thanks for coming."

"And it's taken till now." Ryan Fallon laughed.

"Guess we had to wait until HQ was ready for you," O'Grady said.

"Ready for the two of us. Let's go." He turned towards the cars.

O'Grady hesitated, looking at the river. "Miss Joyce," he said.

Fallon followed his gaze. "The rivers team are on it, after your call. They'll be trawling further downstream. He glanced at O'Grady. "I don't hold out much hope. Come on, fella."

Bobby and Bridie were led to the patrol car. Bobby was less tearful now, and cheered up even more when he was allowed to play with the radio and switch the sirens on and off.

Bridie walked over to O'Grady. She took him in her arms, then turned to Fallon. "Look after him," she said.

O'Grady sat next to Fallon in the unmarked car.

"HQ are expecting me," he said to Fallon.

"They're expecting me too," Fallon said. "Hawthorne was questioned in hospital. He's saying nothing, of course. It's up to us to tell them the truth. And this time they'll listen. They rang me at HQ, asked me to come in. Reckon they need a safe pair of hands."

"They'll get it with you," O'Grady said.

"And you?" Fallon stared at the road ahead, waiting for his answer.

"I can't see they'll be in a hurry to invite me back, Fallon."

"All you've done is put two villains out of the way. And one out of his job. What's not to like?"

O'Grady laughed.

"It'll be a breeze, fella. They'll sit you down in the recording room, and you'll tell them the whole story. End of."

They drove to HQ. Fallon left him in a windowless room with two officers, one male, one female. Microphones were set up, recording devices switched on. They sat opposite him, note-books poised.

He began to talk. He began at the end, with Vera disappearing into the water. He talked about finding Bobby missing, the race to the weir, then, working further back, he told them about the ghost estate, Kiley MacAteer, Sean O'Connor, the inheritance of the land, the need for a water source. He told them about the rape and killing of Maura Salter, and the cover-up at the highest levels. He told them about his investigations when he was still a sergeant, how his work was ignored, overruled. He told them about the death of Gregson Elliott, and that the only fingerprints on the pistol that killed him would be Brian Hawthorne's. He told them where to find the DNA samples he had secretly stored.

They sat, wrote, listened.

He quietened, stopped.

They looked up at him. "And Miss Joyce?" they asked. "We still don't understand. How was it that this upright, moral, elderly lady had intended to kill a six-year-old boy?"

O'Grady took a deep breath. "This is what she told me," he began. And so he went on, told them all about the Green Man, Richard Salter's research, Vera's recreation of the myth.

"But why?" the male officer said. "I still don't understand."

O'Grady hesitated. In his mind, he saw her standing there in the pale dawn light, injured, bleeding, owning her past, telling her pain. He began to speak. "It was like this," he said. And he retold Vera's story, trying to be true to her words, trying to recall all that she'd said, how as a young girl her trust had been so evilly betrayed, how her life had been destroyed.

The two officers sat, listened, scribbled.

At last he got to the end. They looked up from their notes. The woman officer breathed a sigh. "Sounds like a fairy tale," she said. "Except fairy tales have happy endings."

O'Grady smiled. "You haven't read the old ones," he said.

"Well"—she got to her feet—"DI Fallon says you're free to go. On condition that you stay at the address noted here. Given that you've killed two men and injured another. Talking of which, do you want to know how Hawthorne is?"

"Not particularly," O'Grady said.

"He's upstairs," the male officer said.

"He's what?" O'Grady was on his feet.

"Packing boxes," the man said. "He's been sacked, awaiting an investigation into irregularities. The hospital said he wasn't well enough to be discharged, but he checked himself out, insisted on packing the crates in person. Took two of the guys to help him into his office."

O'Grady was by the door, rattling at the locks.

"Where are you going?" The woman officer clicked the door open.

"I still have work to do," O'Grady said.

May Riley on reception greeted him with her sweet smile.

"Aren't you going to try to stop me?" he said. "I'd got rather used to it."

"Me?" She gave a shrug, her pretty head on one side. "I don't care. He's nothing to me now. Security are making him pack his bags. Not a moment too soon."

O'Grady pushed at the door.

Hawthorne was slumped in his chair, surrounded by packing cases. His leg was bandaged. He was wheezing, pasty-faced. He looked up.

"You? What the fuck are you doing here? I can have you arrested for murder."

O'Grady stood in the doorway and laughed. "Kiley Mac-Ateer has gone. O'Connor has gone. Who's going to believe you? Who's going to care?"

Hawthorne's face grew red. He rose from his desk, pushing himself upwards on his hands, tried to step forwards, stumbled and fell. He lay there, helpless, his sparse gray hair in lank threads against the carpet.

O'Grady looked down at him. "Look at you," he said.

"You won't get away with this, O'Grady."

"I've given my statement. About your cover-up, about how you were there when Maura Salter died at the hands of Kiley MacAteer. About your silencing of Gregson Elliott. I've told them where to find the DNA evidence. Ryan Fallon is back."

"Fallon—no one will believe him."

"Really? He has the files, the evidence. It's over, Hawthorne. No one will do your bidding anymore. The Devlin twins have legged it, last seen on their way to Dublin in a stolen Merc."

Hawthorne rocked to and fro, attempting to get up, spitting with rage.

O'Grady went to him, put his arms under the man's heavy form, lifted him up, helped him into his chair.

"There you are." He stepped back and surveyed him. "Do you want to know why I didn't kill you, Hawthorne? The others met their fate. But you—I aimed to maim you, just there." He pointed at the bandaged leg. "You see, I knew this would be worse for you."

Hawthorne wriggled and panted, helpless in his seat.

"You'll be tried, Hawthorne. They'll find you guilty. A long sentence awaits you." O'Grady took another step back, stood in the doorway. "It's your turn now, Brian. All those years to contemplate your sins. As we were taught by the holy sisters."

CHAPTER 30

FALLON DROVE HIM BACK. "Your car's still at the weir—I'll drop you there."

The afternoon had clouded, and a chill wind rippled the trees.

"It's good to see you again, Ryan."

"It's good to be back. My days of exile are over, it seems. They've asked me to take Hawthorne's job. There'll be a bit of politics first, making sure I'm supported by an honest crew, a new team. But everyone seems glad to see the back of him. He'll do time, there's no doubt of that. Years and years, if I have my way."

The river had quietened. It had come on to rain. O'Grady and Fallon stood by the weir, staring at the rush of water.

"We've had the boys out looking, but it's a fruitless task. I know these waterways." Fallon sighed. "She'll come to light in her own time. In days. Weeks, maybe. Body found, miles downstream, caught in some weeds. Maybe still recognizable, with any luck." He turned away, and O'Grady followed him.

At the car, Fallon shook his hand. "I owe you a debt," he said. "A massive debt. You never gave up. As you used to say. Justice. Always worth fighting for."

O'Grady opened the door of his car.

"By the way," Fallon said. "Don't worry about bail conditions. As far as I'm concerned, you're free to go. Although"—he watched as O'Grady got into his car—"looks to me like you're not planning on going anywhere at all."

O'Grady parked his car at the farmhouse. He opened the door quietly.

The first thing he saw was Bobby, sitting in the corner, pushing a toy police car to and fro, making siren noises.

Then Bridie was there in the doorway. She took him in her arms, led him into the warm back room, sat next to him on the sofa. The weariness had left her. Her cheeks were pink, the sparkle had returned to her eyes.

He explained the whole story, the return of Ryan Fallon, the end of Hawthorne. "He's probably still stuck in that chair, raging," he said.

She laughed, shook her head. "They'll have locked him up by now if they've got any sense." She leaned towards him, her hand on his. "And you, love," she said. "No more charges hanging over you."

He gave a nod.

"You could stay," she said. "They could give you your job back."

He met her eyes, and saw in their deep yearning a future for them both.

He was silent.

She wrapped her fingers in his. "We Salters," she said. "We make the same mistakes. My father, bless him, shut himself away, failing to hear the facts beyond his stories. And it turns out, I was just the same. It took you to come here, to open my eyes to the reality. Finn, you saved my child. I owe you everything."

He lifted her fingers to his lips.

"You are a hero," she said. "And you have come home."

They had supper—chicken pie, apple cake—sitting round the table as a family of three. Bobby, subdued, wanted to know when he'd see Nana Vee again, and Teddy Peter, talking in his Ulster voice, had to explain that she'd gone to heaven and was happy there with all the angels. Bobby held his teddy tight and managed a smile.

O'Grady watched the evening pass, aware that he was seeing it as if from the outside. *This was once the life I wanted,* he thought. *Still to be a police officer, with a wife and family. In this warm room is all that I once thought was denied to me.*

At last Bridie persuaded Bobby that it was time to go to bed.

O'Grady went outside, stood in the garden. *Three years ago,* he thought, *if you'd told me that I could once again be an officer in the Garda, with Bridie as my wife, with a little boy too…I'd have thought I'd got it made. But something has happened to me in these years of exile.*

He looked across the valley. He thought about his mother's house, over the hill. He remembered the little yard where he'd once played, brandishing his sword, fighting imaginary knights.

"Finn." Bridie's voice interrupted his thoughts. She came and stood beside him. She took hold of his hand. "One more night," she said. "Perhaps two. And then goodbye."

"But—"

She looked up at him. "Once I broke your heart," she said. "But this time—this time I'm setting you free."

EPILOGUE

"WILL PASSENGERS INTENDING TO board flight six zero three to London Heathrow, please go to gate number eleven."

O'Grady joined the queue. Dublin airport was noisy, busy, bright with horizontal sunlight.

Two days had passed. Now it was Wednesday. He'd left the town that morning. Driven his Audi to the airport and parked it at the car-hire drop-off point.

He'd looked at the car, holding the keys tightly in his hand. He'd surveyed the mud-spattered wheels, the leaves gathered at the base of the windscreen.

Ten days since he'd picked it up. And in that time, a whole story. *Like a fairy tale,* the policewoman had said.

But with no fairy-tale ending.

He'd left Bridie that morning. They'd held each other tight, each holding in their thoughts the memories of their time together, their laughter, their lovemaking.

The queue to board shuffled forward.

And then they'd said goodbye.

"You'll be back," she'd said, smiling through tears. "You'll be an Irishman once more."

He'd kissed her, murmured that he'd always be an Irishman, kissed her again.

And now here he was, queueing for the London flight.

After Heathrow, what next? There'd been emails. A job offer from a company in Manhattan providing bodyguards to the wealthy. A private investigation team in Honolulu trying to put a stop to a very lucrative multinational cocaine ring. There was one from an old friend from the Garda who'd spent the last three years in the Middle East, tracking down a key link in the illegal armaments trade. He pulled out his phone, looked at the message again. "The lads are good craic. And the desert's nice and warm. Not much rain. Makes a change from Connemara…"

The ping of a text arriving. From Ryan Fallon:

Good luck, fella. You know there's a job here for you whenever you want.

It was time to board the plane.

Once more the bright blue sky, the crystalline daylight. O'Grady leaned back in his airplane seat and looked down at the sunlit clouds.

He remembered his mother's words. "You're a restless spirit, Finn. A nomad."

He sipped his plastic cup of Irish whiskey.

There are worse things, he thought.

ABOUT THE AUTHORS

JAMES PATTERSON has written more bestsellers and created more enduring fictional characters than any other novelist writing today. He lives in Florida with his family.

ALISON JOSEPH is a London-based crime writer and award-winning radio dramatist. After a career in television documentaries, she began writing full-time with the Sister Agnes series of crime novels. Alison also writes a police series featuring Detective Inspector Berenice Killick.

MICHAEL BENNETT, BE GRATEFUL YOU'RE ALIVE.

Someone attacked the Thanksgiving Day Parade directly in front of Michael Bennett and his family. The television news called it "holiday terror"—Michael Bennett calls it personal. The hunt is on....

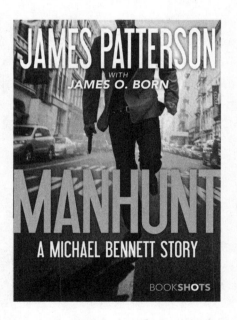

Michael Bennett is back. Read on for a special excerpt from the newest addition to the Bennett series, *Manhunt,* available only from

CHAPTER 1

MY ENTIRE BROOD, PLUS Mary Catherine and my grandfather, gathered in the living room. We'd been told to expect a call from Brian between eight and eight fifteen. That gave us enough time to eat, clean up, and at least start the mountain of homework that nine kids get from one of the better Catholic schools in New York City.

We had the phone set on speaker and placed it in the middle of the group, which was getting a little antsy waiting for the call.

At exactly ten minutes after eight, the phone rang and some dull-voiced New York Department of Corrections bureaucrat told us that the call would last approximately ten minutes and that it would be monitored. Great.

My oldest son, Brian, had made a mistake. A big mistake—selling drugs. Now he was paying for that mistake, and so were we.

Tonight was Thanksgiving eve. Tomorrow we would embark on our annual tradition of viewing the Macy's Thanksgiving Day Parade, and it would hurt not having Brian with us.

My late wife and I had begun this tradition even before we started adopting kids. She'd get off her shift at the hospital and

I'd meet her near Rockefeller Center. When the kids were little, she loved the parade more than they did. It was one of many traditions I kept alive to honor her memory.

She even made the parade after chemo had wrecked her body, with a scarf wrapped around her head. The beauty still managed an excited smile at the sight of Bart Simpson or Snoopy floating by.

As soon as Brian came on the line, there was a ripple in our crowd. The last time I'd seen him, he was still recovering from a knife attack that was meant to send me a message.

Tonight, he sounded good. His voice was clear and still had that element of the kid to it. No parent can ever think of their child as a convicted felon, even if he's sitting in a prison. Currently, Brian was temporarily housed at Bear Hill Correctional, in the town of Malone, in northern New York. It was considered safe. For now. Mary Catherine and I talked over each other while we asked him about the dorm and classes.

Brian said, "Well, I can't start classes because I haven't been officially designated at a specific prison. That will happen soon."

All three of the boys spoke as a group. As usual, they took a few minutes to catch Brian up on sports. Football always seemed to be the same—the Jets look bad, the Patriots look good.

Then an interruption in the programming.

Chrissy, my youngest, started to cry. *Wail* is probably more accurate.

Mary Catherine immediately dropped to one knee and slipped an arm around the little girl's shoulder.

Chrissy moaned, "I miss Brian." She turned to the phone like there was a video feed and repeated, "I miss you, Brian. I want you to come home."

There was a pause on the phone, then Brian's voice came through a little shakier. I could tell he was holding back tears by the way he spoke, haltingly. "I can't come home right now, Chrissy, but you can do something for me."

"Okay."

"Go to the parade tomorrow and have fun. I mean, so much fun you can't stand it. Then I want you to write me a letter about it and send it to me. Can you do that?"

Chrissy sniffled. "Yes. Yes, I can."

I felt a tear run down my cheek. I had some great kids. I don't care what kind of mistakes they might've made.

We were ready for our adventure tomorrow.

CHAPTER 2

IT WAS A BRIGHT, cloudless day and Mary Catherine had bundled the kids up like we lived at the North Pole. It was cold, with a decent breeze, but not what most New Yorkers would consider brutal. My grandfather, Seamus, would call it "crisp." It was too crisp for the old priest. He was snuggled comfortably in his quarters at Holy Name.

I wore an insulated Giants windbreaker and jeans. I admit, I looked at the kids occasionally and wished Mary Catherine had dressed me, as well, but it wasn't that bad.

I herded the whole group to our usual spot, across from Rockefeller Center at 49th Street and Sixth Avenue. It was a good spot, where we could see all the floats and make our escape afterward with relatively little hassle.

I was afraid this might be the year that some of the older kids decided they'd rather sleep in than get up before dawn to make our way to Midtown. Maybe it was due to Chrissy's tearful conversation with Brian, but everyone was up and appeared excited despite the early hour.

Now we had staked out our spot for the parade, and were waiting for the floats. It was perfect outside and I gave in to the overwhelming urge to lean over and kiss Mary Catherine.

Chrissy and Shawna crouched in close to us as Jane flirted with a couple of boys from Nebraska—after I'd spoken to them, of course. They were nice young men, in their first year at UN Kearney.

We could tell by the reaction of the crowd that the parade was coming our way. We sat through the first couple of marching bands and earthbound floats before we saw one of the stars of the parade: Snoopy, in his red scarf, ready for the Red Baron.

Of course, Eddie had the facts on the real Red Baron. He said, "You know, he was an ace in World War I for Germany. His name was Manfred von Richthofen. He had over eighty kills in dogfights."

The kids tended to tune out some of Eddie's trivia, but Mary Catherine and I showed interest in what he said. It was important to keep a brain like that fully engaged.

Like any NYPD officer, on or off duty, I keep my eyes open and always know where the nearest uniformed patrol officer is. Today I noticed a tall, young, African-American officer trying to politely corral people in our area, who ignored him and crept onto the street for a better photo.

I smiled, knowing how hard it is to get people to follow any kind of rules unless there is an immediate threat of arrest.

Then I heard it.

At first, I thought it was a garbage truck banging a Dumpster as it emptied it. Then an engine revved down 49th Street, and I turned to look.

I barely had any time to react. A white Ford step-van truck barreled down the street directly toward us. It was gaining speed, though it must have had to slow down to get by the dump truck parked at the intersection of 49th and Sixth as a blockade.

Shawna was ten feet to my right, focused on Snoopy. She was directly in the path of the truck.

It was like I'd been shocked with electricity. I jumped from my spot and scooped up Shawna a split second before the truck rolled past us. I heard Mary Catherine shriek as I tumbled, with Shawna, on the far side of the truck.

The truck slammed into spectators just in front of us. One of the boys from Nebraska bounced off the hood with a sickening thud. He lay in a twisted heap on the rough asphalt. His University of Nebraska jacket was sprayed with a darker shade of red as blood poured from his mouth and ears.

The truck rolled onto the parade route until it collided with a sponsor vehicle splattered with a Kellogg's logo. The impact sent a young woman in a purple pageant dress flying from the car and under the wheels of a float.

Screams started to rise around me, but I couldn't take my eyes off the truck.

The driver made an agile exit from the crumpled driver's door and stood right next to the truck. Over his face, he wore a red scarf with white starburst designs.

He shouted, *"Hawqala!"*

CHAPTER 3

I STOOD IN SHOCK like just about everyone else near me. This was not something we were used to seeing on US soil.

Eddie and Jane, crouching on the sidewalk next to me, both stood and started to move away from me.

I grabbed Eddie's wrist.

He looked back at me and said, "We've got to help them."

Jane had paused right next to him as I said, "We don't know what's going to happen."

As I said it, the driver of the truck reached in his front jacket pocket and pulled something out. I couldn't identify it exactly, but I knew it was a detonator.

I shouted as loud as I could, "Everyone down!" My family knew to lie flat on the sidewalk and cover their faces with their hands. A few people in the crowd listened to me as well. Most were still in shock or sobbing.

The driver hit the button on the detonator and immediately there was a blinding flash, and what sounded like a thunderclap echoed among all the buildings.

I couldn't turn away as I watched from the pavement. The blast blew the roof of the truck straight into the air almost thirty feet. I felt it in my guts. A fireball rose from the truck.

The driver was dazed and stumbled away as the roof landed on the asphalt not far from him.

Now there was absolute pandemonium. It felt like every person on 49th Street was screaming. The blast had rocked the whole block.

The parade was coming to an abrupt stop. Parade vehicles bumped each other and the marching band behind the step van scattered. A teenager with a trumpet darted past me, looking for safety.

The driver pushed past spectators on the sidewalk near us and started to run back down 49th Street where he had driven the truck.

The ball of flame was still rising like one of the floats. Then I noticed a couple of the floats were rising in the air as well. The human anchors had followed instinct and run for their lives.

Snoopy was seventy-five feet in the air now.

Several Christmas tree ornaments as big as Volkswagens, with only three ropes apiece, made a colorful design as they passed the middle stories of Rockefeller Center.

I glanced around, but didn't see any uniformed cops close. The one young patrolman I had seen keeping people in place was frantically trying to help a child who had been struck by the truck.

I had no radio to call for backup. I just had my badge and my off-duty pistol hidden in my waistband.

There had been plenty of cops early, but now I saw that some of them had been hurt in the explosion, others were trying to help victims. It was mayhem, and no one was chasing the perp. I was it. I had to do something.

CHAPTER 4

WHEN I STOOD UP, my legs still a little shaky, I focused on the red scarf I'd seen around the driver's face and neck as he fled the scene. The splash of color gave me something to focus on.

I looked around at my family, making sure everyone was still in one piece. They were on the ground and I said, "Stay put."

I worked my way past panicked parade spectators until I was in the open street and could see the driver half a block ahead. I broke into a sprint, dodging tourists like a running back.

By this point, no one realized the man running from the scene was the driver. The people this far back on the street didn't have a front row seat to the tragedy. No one tried to stop him. Everyone was scrambling for safety, if there was such a place.

I started to gain on the man because he hadn't realized yet that he was being pursued. He had a loping gate as if one of his legs was injured. But he was also alert, checking each side and behind him as he hurried away.

I wasn't a rookie chasing my first purse-snatcher in the Bronx. I didn't feel the urge to yell, "Stop, police!" I was silent and hung back a little bit so he didn't pick up on me.

He took the corner, then slowed. He looked around, as if he

was expecting someone to meet him. I paused at the edge of a high-end fashion boutique and watched him for a moment. I still hadn't drawn my pistol, to avoid attracting attention.

Finally, the truck driver decided his ride wasn't here and started down the street again. He looked over his shoulder one time as he approached a packed diner, and surprised me by slipping inside.

I looked in the window as I came to the door of the diner. Every patron and server was glued to the TV in the corner of the room. News of the attack was mesmerizing. The room was silent as the news had just broken—the same TV parade footage was on a loop as the newscaster started repeating the information he was receiving. No conversation, no clinking of silverware, nothing.

I immediately stepped to the cashier by the front door, held up my badge, and said in a low voice, "NYPD. Did you see where the man who just came in here went?"

The dark-haired young woman shook her head. She mumbled, "I didn't notice anyone." Then she turned and looked back at the TV.

Even though the attack had happened only a couple of blocks away, a few minutes ago, watching it on TV made it feel like it was another country.

I saw the hallway that led past the kitchen. There was a sign that said RESTROOM, so I presumed a back door was that way as well. I hustled, squeezing past several tables crowded with extra patrons. Today was a big day for New York eateries.

Just as I started to pick up my pace, I heard something behind me and turned. The man I'd been chasing was lowering himself from an awkward position above the door. *What the hell?* It looked like it was out of the movies.

When he dropped to the floor and faced me, I realized he had led me into a trap.

CHAPTER 5

THE TRUCK DRIVER AND I stared at each other for a moment. He had taken off the scarf, having used it to trick me. Pretty sharp.

He was about thirty, with neat, dark hair and blue eyes.

I reached for my pistol.

He reacted instantly and blocked my arm. That was from training. That's not a natural move. Then he head-butted me. Hard. My brain rattled and vision blurred.

I stumbled back and kept reaching for my pistol. Just as I pulled it from under my Giants windbreaker, the man swatted it out of my hand. I heard it clatter onto the hard, wooden floor—then the man kicked it.

The gun spun as it slid across the floor and under a radiator.

The man nodded to me and sprinted away. He didn't want to fight, he just wanted to escape.

I couldn't let that happen.

I was dazed and unable to reach my pistol, but I had to do something. I just put one foot in front of the other and followed the man.

My head started to clear.

A moment later, I found myself in the kitchen. The cooks

and busboys weren't paying any attention to us. They were watching the news, just like everyone else, but on one of their smartphones. The back door wasn't at the end of the hall, like I had expected, but through the kitchen.

The man was almost to the back door when he turned and saw me. He looked annoyed, and he turned his full attention on me and charged forward.

I picked up a bottle of cooking wine and smashed it across his face just before he reached me.

The driver teetered back. Blood poured out of a gash on his cheek. Just as I was about to subdue him so I could call for backup, his foot flew up and connected with my chin.

That was the second time this asshole had made me see stars.

This time he took the opportunity and ran. He was out the door in a flash.

TWO BODIES ARRIVED AT THE MORGUE—AND ONE WAS STILL BREATHING.

A wealthy woman checks into a hotel room and entertains a man who is not her husband. A shooter blows away the lover and wounds this millionairess, leaving her for dead. Is it the perfect case for the Women's Murder Club—or just the most twisted?

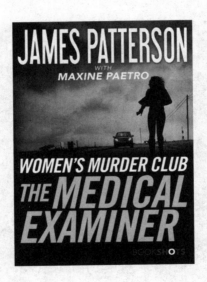

Read the newest addition to the
Women's Murder Club series,
The Medical Examiner, available only from

BOOKSHOTS

DR. CROSS, THE SUSPECT IS YOUR PATIENT.

An anonymous caller has promised to set off deadly bombs in Washington, DC. A cruel hoax or the real deal? By the time Alex Cross and his wife, Bree Stone, uncover the chilling truth, it may already be too late....

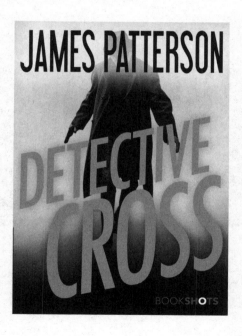

Read the thrilling new addition to the Alex Cross series, *Detective Cross,* **available only from**

BOOK**SHOTS**

BONJOUR, DETECTIVE LUC MONCRIEF.
NOW WATCH YOUR BACK.

Very handsome and charming French detective Luc Moncrief joined the NYPD for a fresh start—but someone wants to make his first big case his last.

Welcome to New York.

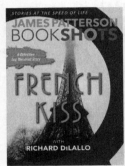
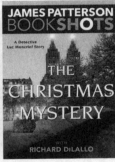
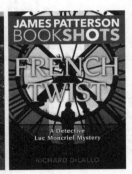

Read all of the heart-pounding thrillers in the Luc Moncrief series:

French Kiss
The Christmas Mystery
French Twist

Available only from

BOOK**SHOTS**